Rainy Days

Rainy Days

Samarth Prakash

GOOD TIMES

GOOD TIMES BOOKS PVT. LTD.
New Delhi (India)
www.goodtimesbooks.com

Published by

GOOD TIMES BOOKS PVT. LTD.
H-13, Bali Nagar, New Delhi-110 015 (INDIA)
Phones: +91-11-25913301, 45069086 Fax: +91-11-45069086
Email : info@goodtimesbooks.com
Website : www.goodtimesbooks.com

First Good Times Edition 2012
Second Good Times Impression 2012
ISBN-13 : 978-93-806194-5-3

All characters and incidents in this novel are fictional. Any resemblance to any person, dead or alive, or resemblance to any organization is purely coincidental...

Typeset in 10.5 pts. Aldine 401BT
by Good Times Design Cell

Printed in India at
Salasar Imaging Systems

Contents

Author's Note

There are a lot of stories in this world, each of them significant in their own small way. Some of them connect to our lives in ways that we cannot fathom; some of them seem to strike a chord somewhere deep inside. This story – perhaps seemingly simple, yet deeply heartfelt – was born in a place inside me where melancholy meets happiness. And because most lives are interesting amalgamations of joy and sorrow, I do wish that this story connects with you in some way.

All the incidents in this book are fictional, yet the feelings are most certainly real. And perhaps some of the true feelings that percolate through the words in these pages will somewhere meld with the true feelings in your heart. Every part of this story, every page of this book, is written in the hope that it will touch some part of you that is yet untouched.

PART ONE

Chapter 1

May 6, 2011

Choices, connections, chance encounters. Destiny has a way of turning even the dullest life into a fascinating tale of trysts and farewells, and of love and doom. It had chosen a murky, slightly confusing day to revisit my past, and perhaps, to define my future. The sprinkling of rain that hit the windshield of my car added to the fuzziness, somewhat blurring my vision of the road that lay ahead.

There's something about the rain and the endless force that it unleashes. There's something about the sound of those drops crashing against the hard earth that rings a bell inside us. There's something about the calm that pervades before the burst, and the silence that forever remains after the deluge. It doesn't quite matter whether that spell of rain brings happiness or sorrow, for both of those much talked about words in the dictionary of life, somewhere along the line dissolve into one.

Trees swayed on either side and the fallen leaves scattered across the road, as I drove on with a constant stream of thoughts running through my mind. At times it seemed like those trees were dancing with joy – in sync – to the music that arose from somewhere beyond, somewhat similar to the tunes that had coloured my life somewhere in the past – a distant musical past that was still faintly audible in the ears of my heart.

It was a normal day for the world, but for me it was almost a day of reckoning. It was promising enough to be the most memorable day of my life. Reunions are memorable, and we have to thank parting for making them possible. But that day also had the potential to deal a decisive blow.

The happiness that had been dormant in me for so long could explode in one moment of dramatic turnaround. Equally, the long pent-up affliction could force itself out. Either way, it was perhaps going to be a day of liberation, maybe of acceptance.

The debate raged on inside me – as it had, ever since she had left me – on whether she would indeed keep her vow of meeting me on this day, after exactly five years. My heart repeatedly affirmed positive thoughts of a beautiful, soft rekindling of romance, but my ever-doubting mind constantly brought up devils that crushed my hope.

The rain intensified into a somewhat thick shower, with the sun nowhere in sight, almost turning the day into night, much like those destined events that take joy in twisting and turning our lives into endless melancholy. The odd car that passed by, seemed to me like sporadic moments of happiness that speed past, almost unspotted, in the midst of the rain that forever drenches us.

I pulled up the windows to stop the rain drops in their quest to enter my car and flood it, much like some of us – in rare moments of strength – try to guard our hearts and minds to keep out the pain that life inevitably brings us. Whether we succeed in our endeavour – like the glass windows of my car – is hard to tell.

I wondered if everything in life is connected, if everything in life signifies something — the rain, the clouds, all those paths that invite us, the people we don't even meet, the windows and doors that we open and close, the constant journeys that we undertake, and those that we don't, the silence, the screams within, the past, the non-existent present, the future, the lines on our hands, the lines on someone else's hands and our destiny that some of us claim we can change.

I trampled those heavy thoughts that further weighed down my heart and trained my mind towards what lay ahead. The road was now completely soaked in water, almost slippery and barely visible.

The train of thoughts inside me returned to the possibilities that the day contained – possibilities that included quenching the thirst of my eyes to see her light again. It was to be a homecoming of sorts for me, for without her my heart had never felt at home. Life had almost been akin to a deep slumber, yet not death. And that middle path, where we are stuck in a state of never-ending confusion, is the worst place to be in. I fervently hoped that I would wake up that day.

I turned into a small, narrow road that had barren land on both sides, as the rain began to show signs of dying down. After driving for two or three miles, I arrived at a favourite place of mine. It was a deserted area on the banks of a small lake. It was a place where she and I had often spent time together; a place where we had shared many moments of indefinable happiness and indeed of bewildering depth.

I parked my car and stepped out. The rain had just about stopped now, and the sky up there seemed to be somewhat clear of clouds. And in the lonely, still rain-filled air that encompassed me, I hoped that the clouds over my life would soon disappear.

There was silence all around, except for the occasional sound of a bird and that of the wind brushing the leaves of tall trees. It was much like the silence that had crept into my life since that unexpected day, now long ago. My thoughts went back to those days with her, those days of almost inexplicable high. Flashes of old days ran past my heart and mind.

The setting seemed to me an interesting amalgamation of joy and melancholy. It's probably true that the outer world is a reflection of our inner world. One moment, I felt joy and hope inside me. Joy, because I would see her after five long years. Joy, because our eyes would meet after such a long time. I would feel the warmth of her embrace again. And the atmosphere seemed perfect for love and reunion. Another moment, fear and anxiety gripped me. What if she did not turn up? What if I could never see her again? And suddenly, the atmosphere seemed to turn dark and sad.

As I remembered the day when I first saw her, the pages of the past – those lovely and splendid days when we were together – opened up before me.

Chapter 2

September, 2005

There was a huge queue of people waiting to enter the stadium. Inside, an intriguing cricket match was about to begin. India and Australia had been part of many closely fought matches in recent times. Naturally, there were elevated expectations from the one day international, especially with it being the decider in a series tied at two all.

The city of Bangalore was all set to witness the spectacle. With its pleasant climate and varied crowd, it was the perfect setting, except for the possibility of rain. I could hear that the toss was about to take place; the crowd inside was going crazy. I cursed myself for being late.

With every cheer that came from inside, the excitement and anticipation of those in the queue grew. Finally, I managed to get in, just as the Indian openers were about to walk out to take strike. I wonder if anything in India can beat the atmosphere of a cricket match. It was electrifying, magnificent, ear numbing. It was stupendous. It raised the expectations to a different level altogether.

Just as I had found a place to settle down, light drops of rain began to fall. Rain is a wonderful thing, as long as it doesn't cause you to get stuck in a traffic jam, and as long as it doesn't pour during a vital cricket match. It was still a light drizzle, not enough to stop the match, and everyone was wishing it away.

The batsmen were ready, fielders had just about taken their positions and the match was a few seconds away from starting. Suddenly, the somewhat light drizzle that had almost disappeared out of contention, stormed back with vengeance. Within a matter of seconds – much like what often happens in life – the match had been ruined. The players walked back without a ball being bowled.

India being India, all spectators waited patiently for the rain to subside. There was no cover over the stand where I was seated, and I opened and held an umbrella over myself. I hated myself for carrying an umbrella as I somehow felt responsible for the rain.

With great disappointment, I looked around and saw a pretty girl sitting next to me. She was holding her handbag over her head to cover herself. As the rain got heavier, it was insufficient to protect her from the rain, and I instinctively moved my umbrella towards her, so that it now covered her head as well. She understandably gave me a weird look, but didn't say anything nor did she push away.

She wore a pink salwar and a dark blue dupatta. Her medium height and fair, average-sized body were a perfect complement to her pretty face. She also wore a longish bindi, which, I felt, somewhat didn't suit her. Ditto for her colourful earrings, which were sort of odd. But then, what did I know of fashion?

Yet she looked simple. She was beautiful. And I was somewhat drawn to her like a person is drawn to his fate or destiny. I simply couldn't take my eyes off her. I had to stop staring and look away when she gave me another strange look.

"What a nice cricket match ruined; bad luck," I said, trying to start a conversation.

She didn't speak, but nodded slightly. I was somewhat irritated. She could certainly have been a little more courteous, but I didn't give up. Which boy gives up so easily when he spots a beautiful girl?

"Hope the rain stops soon," I tried again.

"Yeah," she finally spoke a word, and surprisingly continued, "The forecast says that it won't rain for too long."

I didn't say anything. The ruined cricket match was no longer in my thoughts. A cricket match is fun, but nothing can match up to a pretty girl with a sweet voice, more so if she is a stranger – not even a pulsating cricket match.

"Have you come alone?" I queried.

I knew that it wasn't a great question to put to a girl who was a stranger, but I had to keep the conversation going.

"Yeah. My colleague was supposed to come with me, but she dropped out last minute. So I had to come alone."

The atmosphere around the ground was almost dull now, with the frenzy of the cricket match on hold.

"In fact, I don't watch much cricket. I decided to come since I had nothing else to do," she continued.

In the ruining drops of rain, in the suspended cricket match, in the disappointed faces all around, my heart sensed something destined. The flames that triggered that sense must have risen from somewhere near the pretty girl beside me.

I looked around. Everyone was beginning to get restless as the downpour showed no signs of abating. I turned towards her and was about to speak, when her phone rang.

"...... No ... Megha here ... Sorry wrong number ... No," she hung up.

"Megha?"

"Yes." She nodded and lightened her face with a little smile – something that I was to become crazy about – accompanied by a dimple that took the smile to dizzy heights.

"I'm Raghav," I said. Her smile was still on.

And we continued the conversation, now somewhat beyond the stranger phase. As it often happens, it led to talks about random things and random thoughts, much like the random set of events that had been responsible for the meeting. We started with a little bit of cricket – whatever teeny weeny bit a girl knows about it – and veered to many other topics.

"Have you seen any other cricket match in a stadium?" I asked.

"No, this is my first time. You?"

"Okay. I've come here once before; that match was rained out."

"You shouldn't have come then," she said, and laughed mildly. In the midst of that laughter, her eyes fell on mine for more than a brief period of time. And somewhere in that extended glance, hidden beyond those dark black eyelids, was a spark that was almost a reflection of the sparks in mine. Did I see that then? I don't know for sure. But now, when my eyes travel back to that day in one moment of instant imagination, I do see it, very vividly, almost enough to even melt the years in between.

Do we actually recognize our soul mate in the first fleeting meeting of the eyes, much like what happens in all those unreal movies? Are those unreal dreams and events that fairytales talk about, actually real? Today, when I think of it, I somehow know that there must be some truth in them. For how else can one explain what happened in the days and years that followed?

"Yeah, and I actually prefer watching on TV, with all the nice commentary," I said.

The rain was suddenly showing signs of slowing down, and the air was somewhat filled with a sense of expectation again. There was an announcement that requested the spectators to wait.

"Where are you from?" I queried.

She didn't look like she was from the south.

"I'm from Pune. Are you from Bangalore?"

"Yes."

As we continued talking, I was impressed with the way she spoke and her knowledge of various topics. But she didn't belong to those types of girls who are boastful or empty talkers. She seemed to be balanced, didn't talk too much, but spoke sense. Someone once told me that boys are not attracted to intelligent girls. I don't think that's completely true. Perhaps boys are not attracted to intelligent girls who act overtly smart.

Some players had come out of the dressing room due to sheer boredom, perhaps to get a feel of the environment. The crowd was cheering them. Her cell phone started sounding again. She picked up the call and began talking in a low voice.

After a ten-minute – for me, irritation inducing – conversation, she got up. Those ten minutes seemed to span much more than the two hours that we had been together.

"I have to go. Looks like it won't stop raining and the match is anyway going to be abandoned. It was nice meeting you. Bye."

With that, she walked away. I was somewhat stunned with her sudden departure. I had countless thoughts in my head. "Should I follow her, maybe at least take her phone number or email ID? I don't want to..."

By the time I could gather my thoughts, I could see that she was almost near the nearest visible exit point. Till that point, I hadn't understood the extent of my attraction towards her. Yes, we had just met. The fact that I had thoughts of chasing her might seem somewhat crazy. But that's how it is sometimes. The pull we experience towards someone, the extent to which we like someone is not necessarily a function of the duration of time for which we have known them.

I gathered myself and just ran. By the time I reached the exit point, I could see that she was about to exit the main entrance. I made my way past all the people and commotion. I wanted to call out to her, but was not sure if I should.

When I reached the entrance, she was getting into an auto. I couldn't control myself now and called out her name. But it didn't help, as the auto sped away. I frantically searched for another auto and found one almost immediately. It felt strange to ask the driver to follow another auto, and it seemed as if he too thought the same. But somehow, he didn't question me.

As we followed her, thoughts of destiny came back to me. Maybe, this was a "chosen" day. Maybe, this was a "chosen" path.

As the two autos made their way through the traffic, one following the other, my heart was experiencing a thrill like never before. There's something about chasing a thing in life that makes it even more dramatic and delightful than actually achieving your goal.

All along, I kept an eye on her auto. Suddenly, a car stopped just in front of us. The driver repeatedly tried to restart, but failed. Vehicles stopped on either side of that car for a few seconds, with people just looking on. I egged the driver to go forward.

"Come on, I need to hurry. I don't want to lose sight of that auto. Please go, "I shouted.

We went past the stopped car, but had to halt soon due to a red signal. Thankfully, her auto had also stopped, although it was very close to the signal. I was worried that we would miss her.

As soon as the lights turned green, I shouted again. "Please go, quick."

The auto driver sensing that I really needed to catch that other auto, hurried past the slower moving vehicles – yes, some people do go slower than autos. I have always wondered why some people in vehicles capable of good speed drive extremely slowly in the middle of the road. It irritates me no end. Perhaps one always feels that everyone else drives either too fast or too slow. But nobody's perfect, and I must admit that I have my share of flaws.

Anyway, we crossed the signal just before it turned red again. Even though it was a thrilling ride, it was frustrating in equal measure, with slow moving cycles and two wheelers, "L"-board cars and lost-in-thought drivers. But perhaps all of those added to the thrill. Imagine if the road was empty except for the two autos chasing each other; it would have been a drag.

Finally, I could see her auto stop near a huge building. She stepped out and was walking away. I stopped my auto, paid the driver and ran desperately. By the time I could reach the building, she had gone inside.

The security guard at the gate refused to allow me to enter without an identity card or some referral. All the thrill of the chase disappeared from my system as disappointment took its place. I looked up at the building. There was a board with a list of companies. I guessed that she worked for one of them, though I was not sure why she had gone into the office on a Sunday.

I waited there for some time, with the guard constantly giving me suspicious looks. I hoped that she would come out soon. "Eventually, she has to come out," I thought.

Minutes passed. The wait turned into an hour. Of course I did not know then, that this was just the beginning of the wait. I did not know then, that much longer waits awaited me. It was late evening when I finally gave up. With an assurance that I could always come back some other day, I left.

Even though my home was more than five kilometres away, I decided to walk. I wanted to enjoy the pleasant evening atmosphere and reflect back on the day. The rain had almost completely stopped. It was a wonderful and enjoyable walk and various, mostly positive, thoughts ran through me. As I neared home, night was descending on the city, and lights were slowly being turned on all over.

I am an instinctive person for the most part. It has, on most occasions, brought positive results in my life. Thinking too much doesn't help. But whether that instinctive decision of mine to go after her would indeed bring colour into my life or regret, only time would tell.

I heard later that a twenty over–a side–match had taken place, and Australia had won in a thrilling chase. But I doubt if it was as thrilling a chase as mine.

Chapter 3

My mom's loud calls woke me up the next morning. It was already half past ten, and I had to attend an important meeting in thirty minutes. I hurriedly got ready and rushed out, ignoring my mom's shouts to eat something before leaving. My office was a temporary arrangement in my friend's house, and was just about five minutes away by walk.

When I got there, everybody was preparing for the meeting. Shantanu's was a big house, and he had converted part of it that had a back entrance into an office setup. We had managed to set up separate desks for each of us and had even fit in a small meeting room.

"Raghav, why are you so late? Mr Simon will be in any minute," Sachin said, as I entered our makeshift office.

"Sorry, I overslept. Is everything ready?"

"Almost. We were just checking the presentation one final time," Shantanu called out, as Sandeep looked on seriously.

Sachin, Shantanu and Sandeep were my closest friends from school, and we had got together after studying in different colleges to start our own company. If you want to be an entrepreneur, believe me when I say that the best time to jump in is straight out of college. Once you are in a routine job for too long and get used to that kind of life, it's hard to switch – or so I've heard. I've known people who could never quite get down to doing what they wanted to do after a few years in a job. And so, with all those considerations, we had decided to give it a shot. It had been more than a year since we had begun.

We were building an online platform through which real stories – even those important stories that may not get significant space elsewhere – could be told, in a different, more appealing way. It was somewhat like an internet channel showcasing various stories, some of which could be news items, narrated through rich media, videos, events, timelines, associated people – some of them linked to other stories – and so on.

It's strange how many stories and people are connected to each other in a way that none of us can fathom. We didn't quite start with the idea of bringing that out, but somewhere along the way it was bound to show up. And once we sensed that, we adapted our platform to highlight those connections.

Whatever we did, along with making it big, we wanted to have a social impact. We had worked hard to get an initial version of the website working. We had also got a few part-time journalists and enthusiastic college students to help us in preparing content.

I was mainly responsible for the content. The others, more technology-oriented than me, worked endlessly to build the entire website infrastructure and various tools, so that media-rich stories could be created easily and made quickly accessible to people.

Sachin was the random-idea generator in the team. He could come up with new ideas almost instantly. Some of them were too weird to even think about, some were quickly shot down by others and some of them were truly good. He was also the artist and the main driving force behind the great looking and attractive website that we had managed to build.

Shantanu was the problem solver. He could find innovative solutions to any problem that we came across. He was a little lazy though, and we had to constantly push him.

Sandeep was a quiet kind of person who believed in just getting work done. He could sit continuously for hours or days together to build something that excited him.

We had managed to get some of our friends and families to start visiting our website. Some of them had spread the word to other people, and we had a decent number of hits every day. For want of finding or agreeing upon a really good name, we had initially named it "RS3" for obvious reasons. And that name stuck.

Mr Simon was a potential investor, who had earlier shown interest in investing in our company. We needed it. We couldn't continue for too much longer without money flowing in. Also, his experience in media – he had been an editor in a media company – could help us. He had already talked to us a few times earlier and wanted to have a final discussion.

He arrived five minutes past the scheduled meeting time. He was a tall, well-built man in his mid-forties, with a slightly squarish face. His scalp only had a few strands of hair.

The meeting went on, with Mr Simon asking us plenty of questions. Finally, after a couple of hours of intense discussion, he seemed to be happy.

"Good job boys. I think you do have something good here, and I am excited to work with you."

"Thank you. We are excited too."

"Will give you the details very soon. We'll meet again."

We were really happy with the outcome and thanked him again, as he took our leave. We spent the afternoon discussing future plans. We had done reasonably well so far. Time had come to take it to the next level, and we sensed that we were ready.

"Things are looking bright," Sachin said, as we finished our discussion.

"Yeah, we seem to be on the right track, though it's early days yet," I said.

"Yeah, we've worked hard to get here, but we'll have to work even harder now."

"Hard work is great, as long as we're enjoying it," Shantanu said.

"If we keep going, I'm sure we'll make it big one day," Sachin predicted.

"Yes, we're all confident of that. But we need to only do our best. We need to put in everything we have. The rest is just destiny," I said, philosophically.

"I don't believe in destiny," Shantanu said.

"Yes, we make our own destiny," Sachin agreed.

"Well yeah, we all sort of said the same thing. I meant that if we concentrate on doing our best, we will get to where we want."

We often slipped into these discussions of our future, and of destiny and philosophy. It was a welcome break from our work, and gave us a different perspective.

The next day, I had to meet to a social activist, Mr. Ranjan Shetty, who had worked relentlessly to expose corruption. I had met him at a public gathering a few days ago. He was impressed with what we were doing and had agreed to help us in whatever way he could. In return, we were going to allow him to use our online channel to put across his thoughts and take it to the people. It was to be a mutually beneficial association.

He was to reveal to us a scandal that involved major, high profile people in the state government. It was, according to him, bigger than any other scandal that had ever happened before. Needless to say, huge sums of money and the like were at the heart of it.

We needed some fresh and astonishing news to spice up our portal. Not that such scandals are greatly surprising anymore. These days, we have almost come to expect corruption. But we hoped that showcasing it differently would make it interesting, along with making an impact. Our intention, though, wasn't to make a story out of anything merely to get publicity. We wanted to publish only what we felt was true and appropriate.

As the clock struck five, I suddenly remembered that I had planned to try my luck outside Megha's office again. I set off, somewhat unsure of whether I really wanted to go. Throughout the ride, I remembered the chase. I had no idea about her timings and decided to wait outside her office for a while.

I didn't see her that day either. I trudged back home, knowing that this was going nowhere. Along the way, I was full of questions. What was I thinking? What was I chasing? Were we not destined to meet again? Were our paths destined to cross just once in this lifetime?

Chapter 4

The gates of Mr. Ranjan's bungalow opened into a slightly crooked, somewhat narrow pathway. I walked along, escorted by the large spaces of lush green grass on either side. The bungalow itself was majestic, its elegance almost resembling an ancient mini castle, yet the architecture most certainly new age.

A young man greeted me as I entered the house. I introduced myself, and he escorted me past a handful of people, into a more private part of the house.

"Please be seated here. Mr Ranjan will join you in a few minutes," he said, and left.

I looked around. The interiors were exquisitely done, with colourful paintings adorning almost every wall. One of them, a lengthy portrait of a traditionally dressed lady with folded hands and probing eyes, stood out, even amongst the other glittering pieces of art. The contrast between the dark coloured sofa sets all around and the perfect white walls added to the feeling of class. Every part of the place almost sparkled with cleanliness. It was, from what I had gathered in the short time I had spent with him, a reflection of the type of person Mr Ranjan was: august, glittering, posh, yet somehow simple and clean.

I settled down on the sofa waiting for him to come and talk to me. Even though he was a social activist, he had made enough money for himself. He had once been a business man, who had initially taken to social work part-time. But it had drawn him so much, that he had left his business to his brother and had become an activist full-time. But he had acquired everything – as he often mentioned – "through all the right means."

Fifteen minutes later, I saw him walking towards me, wearing a long shirt and cotton trousers. He must have been just past fifty, but looked a lot younger.

"All set?"

"Yes sir."

"What do you want to start with?" he asked.

"Sir, do you mind if I do a video recording of our conversation?"

"Not at all."

I stood up and placed my video camera in position, the screen covering almost the length of his frame.

We spoke at length, first about his life in general, and then about the scandal in particular. It was the first time that I had had an opportunity to spend an extended duration of time with him.

"Sir, what drove you to be a social activist?"

"Well, I was a normal person, leading a normal life with family, business and the other fine things that we enjoy. But somewhere along the line, I began to realize that life is probably much more than all that. I began to realize that I – along with the people themselves – had the power to solve peoples' problems, if I wanted to. And so, I started taking up small causes, doing whatever I could to have a positive impact. I started raising my voice."

"But I can see that you enjoy all the pleasures of life even now."

"Yes. That's one message I want to send out, especially to the youth of today. You don't have to give up anything in order to make a difference in others' lives. By all means, pursue your career, pursue material wealth and every other thing that you feel will bring you joy, but you have to pledge to spend some of your time reaching out to people."

"And by helping, I don't mean donating money and such other things, though those are good. I mean dedicating part of your time and using your intelligence to change society for the better. I just mean thinking about the larger world outside your own."

“Yes, that's so well said. It's really important to put this message across to people.”

“And it's also important that your life is the message; not just your words, but your life – everything you do, your work, your personal life, your social life.”

I had always wanted to lead my life the right way, and I believe that those encounters with Mr Ranjan further influenced my thinking. Every seed of thought needs nurturing, and not all of it can come from within.

We moved on to discussing the case of corruption that he wanted to expose. I didn't know too much about it yet, and he did all the initial talking on the topic, my questions merely prodding him on. He also took me inside to his personal space and gave me a few related documents that would add to the power of the story.

"In order to portray anything in the right way, you must understand the entire story,” he said, handing me a sheet of paper that seemed to contain some important information.

"We always do a thorough study before putting together any story."

He looked at some file on his table and shook his head slightly, before keeping it aside. Even though he was there with me, sometimes it felt as if he was somewhere else, in some other world, his mind switching relentlessly between various different thoughts.

“Sir, I'm curious why you didn't take this story to a popular television news channel,” I said, unsure of whether I should have brought that up.

“I have done that in the past for other stories. But I think they tend to sensationalize it in a way that’s quite unnecessary. The hype dies down after a time. I want to bring it out differently this time and see how it works. Anyway, they'll find out soon.”

I nodded, gathering my thoughts, looking down at my notepad. My mind was already sketching out ways to present the story. The plan was to initially write about the scandal only, without revealing specific names, even keeping parts of it hidden. Mr Ranjan would then push the government to conduct a probe, slowly building up support from various quarters. We would continue to add to the story in phases, depending on how things panned out.

“I'll start an agitation once the story is out. We'll see how to take it forward from there.”

“Yes.”

"Also, let me know if you get queries from anyone. I'll handle them.”

"Sure."

After that, we had a general chat, which always happened when we were together. He usually steered the conversation into funny and sometimes personal topics, and perhaps, it brought us closer to each other.

As I left his bungalow and walked back to office, a few uncertain thoughts crowded my mind. Was RS3 on the right track? Did it have the makings of something big? Could we really make something happen? Do dreams really come true? And then I remembered my policy of not dwelling too much on anything. So I just decided to play my part, let things unfold slowly, and not strain myself on the eventual outcome. Thankfully, it crushed the doubtful vibrations that had begun to crop up inside me.

Chapter 5

Back in office, I began putting together elements of the story, translating bits and pieces from the notepad, the video and my mind into a more concrete form. For the next hour or so, I was lost in the specifics of that story and my conversation with Mr Ranjan. The small cup of coffee that lay almost untouched on my desk had turned cold when I found myself again.

Shantanu and Sandeep were dedicating their time to cooking up some handsome new features and services. After Mr Simon had agreed, in principle, to the investment, we were going all out to turn this into something big. The fulfilment of our dreams – even though a long way away yet – seemed to draw nearer, with each passing day.

Though most of our website centred on the main stories that we published and the feedback from people, we had a section where people could narrate their own stories using various tools we had built. As much as possible, everything was moderated. We also intended to periodically feature well-known people in various fields in some of our stories.

We were aware that we couldn't do everything. Our endeavour was to empower the people to do what we wanted to do. Of course, in this age of the Internet and a seemingly smaller world, there are plenty of channels for people to express their opinions. Our frequent discussions revolved around what we needed to do to differentiate our platform.

I had somehow thought that noble intentions and commercial interests could never go together. We had had our share of debates about the topic. But considering the direction in which we were moving, a new sense of hope had descended upon us.

"I've got an optimised version of the video streaming working. We should now be able to support more video traffic, at least 3X," Sandeep called out, excitedly.

The rare outward expression of excitement that came from him drew the rest of us to his desk. He was looking at the results of the tests he had run. We had been worried that our site would crash if the traffic to our website was to increase significantly, especially streaming of videos. Sandeep had been working on finding better hosting options, optimizing and tuning the video streaming.

"Great job! We can now go ahead with more confidence," Shantanu said.

We sat down together and went through some of the stuff we were planning to do. This part, where we ideated and discussed together was what we enjoyed the most, and it most definitely played an important part in our progress.

"We need to generate content faster now. We are almost on track with respect to technology," Sachin thought aloud.

"Yes, we should get in more people once we get the investment from Mr Simon. We need more hands on the job. Any news from him?" I queried.

"Not yet, but we should hear very soon. He's pretty happy with what we've got."

“How much money do you think he'll put in?” I asked

“Don't know for sure, but the hint I got was that it will be more than a decent amount.”

“Enough for a year?”

“Sufficient, I should think. Though it all depends on how we grow.”

“Yeah.”

We returned to our individual desks and got down to finishing what we had to do. Ideas are great, planning is great, but sometimes we forget that execution is equally essential and perhaps one of the chief differentiators between those who become successful and those who don't.

After some more time of intense thought, I had a good draft write-up and sketch ready for the story. Just as I was contemplating taking a break, my thoughts shifted to Megha.

"Guys, I need to go. I have to meet someone. Can you please put together the document that Mr Simon wanted?"

"Whom do you have to meet? Business meeting?" Sachin asked.

"Personal."

"Personal? Girlfriend?" Shantanu asked, as all of them stared at me.

"C'mon, no. When I have a girlfriend, I'll let you guys know. I'm going to meet a friend from college."

"Okay, enjoy yourself."

I had decided that I would go to Megha's office in the afternoon, hoping to catch her if she came out sometime during the day. In fact, I did not even know if she actually worked there. I knew that it was like shooting in the dark, but I had to try something. Thoughts of her had constantly occupied my mind ever since I had met her two days ago.

"One final time," I thought. I understood that it was useless to wait everyday for a stranger in front of some building that I assumed was her office. Why was I actually chasing her? Had I fallen in love with her in just one meeting? It was crazy. But perhaps, it was worth one last attempt.

Chapter 6

It was past one in the afternoon, and I waited outside Megha's supposed office. The occasional rays of light that sneaked through the heavy cloud cover above, built up rushes of hope in me, only to be crushed soon after by the slight movement of those dark floating bodies. I had almost given up hope of finding her, when I saw her walk out of the gates and away from where I was standing. I was filled with some unknown joy and a bout of nervousness, and almost couldn't think. I walked quickly towards her and slowed down when I was just behind her. Unsure of how to approach it, I just called out to her.

"Hi Megha."

She turned around and was definitely surprised to see me there.

"Hey hi."

"Remember me?"

"Yes."

"I was passing by and noticed you."

"Okay, do you work somewhere nearby?"

"No, why?"

"Just like that, what are you doing here then?"

"I was...," I struggled for a bit before continuing, "... visiting a friend."

"Okay."

"Yeah. Anyway doesn't matter why or how I landed up here, it's good to meet you again."

"Ummm... yeah."

"You work here?"

"Yeah."

"Where do you stay?"

"What?"

"Sorry, never mind. Where are you going?" I asked.

I was really nervous talking to her and it was showing on my face and in my words.

"You are asking me so many questions!"

I laughed.

"I thought it was normal to ask questions when we meet someone new."

"I am going home for lunch. I stay nearby and there's not much work today."

"You stay with your parents?" I asked.

"No, I am from Pune, remember? My parents stay there. I just work here."

"You're going to have lunch alone at home?"

"Yeah," she nodded.

"Why? You don't eat with others at your workplace?"

"I do sometimes, but I don't really have too many friends, even at work. I prefer being alone. I'm not much of a social person."

That statement of hers was not too encouraging, but I hoped that it only meant that she was not proactive in making friends.

"Okay, I have an idea. Why don't we have lunch together today?"

"What?"

"Yeah, why not?" I tried to urge her.

"But I hardly know you. How can I have lunch with a stranger?"

"C'mon, we are not strangers anymore; we've already met once. And weren't all our friends, at one time, strangers to us."

That seemed to make a difference, and she smiled.

"I don't know why I'm agreeing to this. Okay, let's go."

Perhaps people who are loners don't really want to be alone. Perhaps it's just that they haven't yet met people who can match their wavelength.

As we walked on, I noticed that she was wearing a dark green salwar and a white dupatta. She had left her hair loose, unlike the time when I first saw her. And, needless to say, she looked even more beautiful.

I was already beginning to think that I had some sort of feelings for her. And even though she didn't seem too excited to see me, I knew that she wouldn't have agreed to come with me if she did not somewhere deep down inside have good thoughts about me. It's not much, I know. But every great feeling, every great story, has small beginnings.

And girls are like that. They always seem to hide something. They never show their true feelings or express their innermost thoughts easily, especially to people they haven't known for too long. I guess they are made that way.

We walked to a restaurant nearby and took our place in a corner. After we had placed the order, and I had endured about two or three minutes of silence, I tried to get a conversation going.

"Strange that we should meet twice in a few days."

"Yeah." She smiled.

"Actually..."

"Actually?"

"Actually, it's no coincidence this time. I came to meet you."

Even though I had wanted to refrain from revealing that to her, I couldn't resist. It had the potential to ruin everything.

"What? What do you mean?"

"I mean... I mean I came to meet you."

"Why?"

I couldn't quite come up with a reply to that question of hers.

"How did you find my office?" she asked.

"I followed you that day after you left the stadium, and saw you entering your office building."

"Huh? You followed me? You are dangerous."

I started laughing.

"Why did you follow me?"

"Every question doesn't have an answer," I said.

"What? I can't believe that you followed me. It's strange."

"What's so strange in a boy following a pretty girl?"

I knew that that was the first vocal complement I had given her. To my relief, she just smiled one of her dimple-filled smiles. I wonder if there is an easier way to impress a girl than praising her external appearance.

“Where do you work?” I asked.

She told me that she worked in a software firm, and from what I gathered from the brief explanation of her work, it seemed to be a dull job.

Our conversation again veered on to various directions, the details of which are not really significant, except that those early conversations with her – words and pauses included – were at the heart of our fond beginnings and will always have a special place in the diary of our lives.

“Why did you go away so quickly that day from the stadium?”

“Oh that day, there was an issue at work and my manager called me. So I had to go.”

“On a Sunday?”

“Yes,” she shrugged her shoulders, “and you followed me.”

"Not only that, but I also waited outside your office for more than an hour. And I even came there the next day."

"Really? My God! You just met me two–three days ago."

I just looked at her. Even though they don't show it, girls are really happy when someone chases them or waits for them.

“This is getting more and more surprising. You better tell me what else you did.”

“That's it. I didn't do anything more,” I said, and laughed, as she added to it with a mild one herself.

“But why?” she asked again.

“Why didn't I do anything more?”

“Why did you wait for me?”

Before I could find a reply, as if she had guessed that I was about to repeat my old answer, she said, “Not every question has an answer, I know.”

"Right."

She shook her head slightly, before taking a sip from the glass of water in front of her.

"What do you do?" she asked after a while.

"My friends and I have started a company. We've come up with a web-based platform that can be used to narrate stories in a more interesting and appealing way. It's called RS3.com."

"Wow, that's interesting. Not bad eh. I'll definitely check it out."

"Yes, you must. Let me know what you think about it."

"I will," she said, nodding her head.

Our food was served. I suppose she was quite hungry; she quickly sunk her teeth into it and seemed to be enjoying every bite. In between gulping down what was on my plate, I kept stealing glances at her, and she caught me staring at her eyes more than once. With every minute we spent that day, the attraction towards her grew.

It was a noisy place, and the din and commotion somewhat drowned our voices. But it couldn't dim the obvious music that played in my heart. And in the neatly crafted, maybe even somewhat confused glances that she gave me, I could see some light in her as well.

After we were done, I paid – even though she was extremely reluctant to allow me to pay the complete amount – and we walked out.

"What time do you usually leave for home after work?" I asked, as we were walking back to her office.

"Around six. Why?"

"So that I can visit you." I smiled.

Her expression was a mixture of a smile and a frown.

"I'll be outside your office at six tomorrow."

"What? Are you planning to meet me every day? Anyway, not tomorrow, we can meet some other day maybe."

"Well, okay. How will I know when you want to meet me?" I asked, hinting that we should exchange phone numbers.

We stopped, as we had reached her office building.

"You chased me, waited outside my office two–three times and then found me. So you'll somehow find out I suppose. And no phone number today." She smiled. It was as if she had sensed my thoughts and wanted to stop them in their tracks.

"Okay, hopefully will see you soon."

She entered the gates and I kept looking at her till she disappeared into the building.

It was late afternoon and there was a hint of rain in the air. Romantic thoughts made their way into my heart: thoughts of Megha, thoughts of love, thoughts of that indefinable space that it leads us to. I had always dreamt of love, especially of the love that happens suddenly, perhaps in one fairytale moment. As the heavens still resisted from opening up fully and the wind gathered momentum around me, I wondered if those dreamy sketches of mine were being filled with colourful reality.

Chapter 7

"I called you twice, where were you?" Sachin asked, as I came back to office.

"I told you that I had to meet a friend. Why, what happened?"

"Mr Simon's secretary had called. She said that they will be making a sizeable investment. We should expect to receive an email tomorrow."

"That's great news!" I said, excited with the prospect of finally having an investor on board.

"Yes, though we sort of knew it, this confirms it. And the key word here is sizeable."

"Yes."

"Anyway, we have the document ready, let's review it."

"Okay."

We settled down – with a cup of coffee – and went through the whole document, including all the statistics, figures and projections. We didn't want to goof up or put in something that was very visibly wrong. It's very easy to make small mistakes, and sometimes, they cost you a lot.

"This looks all right now."

"Have we missed anything?" Sachin asked, as I was giving final touches to the document.

"No, we've got everything covered, I think."

"Yeah."

After that, I was busy with further work on Mr Ranjan's story. When the initial version was ready, we all took a look at the whole thing. We felt that it had shaped up well. It seemed to be a very dramatic narration. It was the first real piece of news that we had.

But we also knew that we needed to find different types of stories. We didn't want to be typecast. We did have fresh ideas of what would make interesting stories, but it was also true that RS3 needed to be much more than just that. We had to be the platform for people to bring out their own stories, to make them feel that their tales could reach out to others, and perhaps actually make a difference.

It was late night and we were all about to leave office, when we received the email from Mr Simon. He had indeed made a big investment, certainly bigger than we had expected. We all read through the email and then shouted in unison, with even Sandeep joining us. That had become a sort of "true" indicator for us, because he usually remained quiet.

"Finally, something significant!" Sachin remarked.

"It's an important milestone, our first investor."

"This in itself is such an amazing feeling, I can imagine what it will feel like when we achieve bigger things," Shantanu said.

I wonder why we always think about the future and bring ourselves under pressure instead of just enjoying the present moment. But I guess we need to have one eye on our long-term goals.

We were in Mr Simon's office the next day to finalize the deal. As we sat there, we had still not realized the magnitude of the part this was to play in our future success. It takes time for big happenings to sink into our minds.

We could now plan for bigger things, with the knowledge that we had the resources to help us get there. With more money came more resources, but also more hard work. With more resources and work came more power, and with it came more responsibility.

I thought about random things. I thought about people – people who help us along the way to success, people who take us with them through our struggles. I only wished that we never forget them when we eventually get there, and more importantly, give something back by reaching out to other people. Life is a chain of connected events, and we all have to play our part in keeping the chain going.

Chapter 8

I did not visit Megha the next day. Sometimes, it's good to make a girl wait for you. Two days later, with the shadows of another pleasant evening just about taking over the light of day, I stood in the now almost familiar position outside her office once again. The fact that she had been somewhat hesitant to meet again played on me, but I somehow saw that in a positive light, because it seemed to me that it was just that – hesitancy – and not disinterest. And I felt that somewhere in the corner of her mind she was anticipating the meeting.

It was over twenty minutes before she came out. She spotted me and came straight towards me.

"Hi."

"Hi! You didn't come yesterday?" she asked.

"No, I thought you told me not to come."

"Since you had said you would come, I waited here for some time."

"What? Really? That's why we should have exchanged phone numbers. You could have called me then."

"Smart eh!" she smiled.

I laughed.

“Actually, I was only talking to someone here, so I just looked around for you. I didn’t wait for too long as such,” she tried to hold back as usual.

“God!” I thought, “Can’t she make up her mind on which way she wants to go?”

I stared at her, the question in my eyes almost seemingly appearing in her heart in an instant. Whether or not her heart had an answer, I couldn't quite make out.

"Let's go somewhere," I said.

We walked to a nearby cafe. It was called S'adonner, a French word that means something like "addicted" or "intoxicated". I didn't dwell too much on that name at the time. I didn't know then that it was to have such significance in my life. I didn't know then that I was to become intoxicated with her love.

I hadn't imagined that it would be this easy to get a chance to win her over. I wasn't completely there yet, but I seemed to be going in the right direction.

"How was your day today?" she asked, in the midst of tying up her loosely hanging hair.

It's those small things about girls that make guys go crazy. Those hands moving through the back of their hair, the tiny, sometimes confused, movement of the lips, the hint of smile that lights up their faces and our lives, those... I could go on and on endlessly.

"How was your day?" she repeated.

"It was good... I think. Yours?"

"Normal," she said. "Which means boring, by the way," she added.

"Why? Don't you like your work?"

"Well, it's all right. There's nothing exciting about it, but it pays me enough for now."

"Yeah, but you should do what you like. I know it's not easy, but at least I'm trying," I said.

"Hmmm... but I don't have any high aspirations."

"Why? You are an intelligent girl. Why don't you have a high ambition?"

She laughed. "I'm not sure I can believe you right now, because you'll obviously say good things about me."

"No, I mean it."

"I don't know. When one comes from a typical lower middle class family, sometimes it doesn't even occur to you that you can dream big. Even if you do, you don't really follow them," she said, with slightly lower than usual voice.

"Hopefully, I'll change your thinking," I said.

She smiled again for the umpteenth time.

"Looks like you are a dreamer."

"Is there anything in life that is better than a dream?"

"I've nothing against dreamers, but I think you people get too carried away. Life is lived in everyday routine, in the struggle every moment. It's not lived in dreams."

I stared at her, at her eyes, at the depth in her eyes. I stared at her picture perfect face. This time, I didn't steal a look; I did it more directly. She stared back for a few moments and then looked away again.

"In a way, you're right. But people who have really achieved something big in life are those who have had dreams and high aspirations," I said, after I had recovered from a bout of dizziness from absorbing her beauty.

"Yeah."

"Anyway, this talk is getting too heavy."

We both laughed mildly, and then, there was silence for a few moments. I couldn't quite believe that I was sitting there with her; it could well have been a dream. Imagine meeting a pretty girl at a cricket match that is ruined due to rain, following her, and taking her out for lunch two days later. And there we were, sitting at S'adonner, indulging in each other's eyes.

"This cannot not be real," I thought.

But it was. However much life saddens us with those long phases of unbearable melancholy, making us feel that reality is miserable and dreams impossible, it does bring to us some rare moments of real joy. Maybe there are fairytales in life after all. But then, I did not realize that a fairytale beginning does not guarantee a smooth ride.

"Where should we go next?" I asked.

"Huh?"

“I assume we are going to meet again?”

“Hmm… maybe,” she shrugged her shoulders.

“You don’t want to?”

“I’m not sure where this is going. Somehow, it makes me tense.”

“Why are you so hesitant about everything? We don’t always know where we are going. Sometimes, we just have to go along.”

She just stared at me. I don’t know what I saw in those eyes. Was it hesitation? Was it confusion? Was it some kind of attraction? Or maybe it was a mixture of everything.

“Where do you want to take me?” she asked, as if somewhere far away, in her heart, the tide had turned from hesitation to desire.

"Where do you want to go?" I asked, after a few moments.

"How about a long drive?" she queried.

"Wow!" I silently thought as I looked at her, “That was totally unexpected.”

Having been a romantic at heart – almost ever since I was born – a long drive with her was already on my mind. Even then, I'm sure I wouldn't have proposed that so quickly. And the fact that she had asked for it herself, made it somewhat more romantic.

I had noticed that she was always reluctant until pushed. But I brushed aside thoughts of her initial hesitant ways and chose to ignore it. I don’t know how different it would have been if I had given more ear or eye or heart to that reluctance of hers. I don’t know if it would have changed anything. It probably didn’t matter. Love is the only thing that matters sometimes.

“What did you say?”

She looked at me with a strange expression.

"How about a long drive??" she repeated her question.

"How long?"

"What? Maybe we can go somewhere where you haven't gone before. I like exploring unknown places."

"Okay, we'll find a new place."

After a pause she said, "Can you stop staring? This is a public place."

"What? Where else can I stare at you?"

She threw a crumpled tissue at me, as we both smiled. We finished sipping our coffee, and just as we were about to leave, I scribbled my phone number on a piece of paper and handed it to her.

"What's this?"

"It's my phone number. I won't ask for yours now, but you can call me when you want to."

She smiled her dimple-enriched smile, again. It melted me no end – that smile of hers. I then walked with her to her house.

"You stay alone?"

"No, my friend stays with me."

"Okay."

I kept looking at her as she stepped into her house and turned around. I took out my phone and held it up to her, to indicate that I would be waiting for her call. She stared at me for a few moments, before shutting the door.

The night had taken over the city, pushing the evening into the past and into our memories, as I made my way back home. But perhaps, all that night, and days after that, I was still there, outside her house, watching her close the door on an indelible evening. Somewhere though, I knew that her heart was beginning to open.

The seeds of something deep were being sown. I didn't know then how far this would go. I didn't know then that the roots would go deep into my heart and firmly entrench themselves. I didn't know then that pulling them out would hurt no end.

Chapter 9

Mr Ranjan's story, combined with his attempts to publicise it, had increased the number of visitors to our website significantly. It was the sort of push that we needed. We had to take this opportunity and convert it into something substantial. In the first few days, the story – replete with a detailed account of what "we thought" had happened, with all those graphic-enriched media, and the interview – had plenty of views, and many people posted comments and talked about it. But we needed to hold them there. We needed to make them come back. More importantly, we needed to channel the power that they had to drive something useful.

In the days just after we published that story, we were put under pressure from various sources to take it off RS3. Mr Ranjan, as promised, handled it perfectly, even sending some of his people to our office when required, and more importantly using other mediums to divert attention away from us to the main point that needed to be made. He had his connections, even political, and we somehow tided over that phase without pulling out the story.

In the following weeks, we launched quite a few new stories, some of them inspirational stories of success, some of them about people who needed help, some of them about people who had dared to try bizarre things, some of them about similar scandals and some of them just pure fun. We also planned to feature a few cities and towns – some well known, some tucked away in remote parts.

And in the process of taking these stories to the people, I realized that the world had so many hidden anecdotes, so many stories that had to be told. And somewhere along the line, my life became integrated into those stories and lives.

More and more people in India were beginning to spend time on the Internet, and this was our chance. Every medium has its own advantages and challenges, and for us to succeed we had to be aware of them.

The makeshift office was no longer sufficient. We needed to move to a new, much larger, space. We had been looking for one, and had narrowed in on a medium-sized space that we thought would be enough for the better part of two years. We revisited the place after we were sure of the investment.

"Good enough," I said, after we had seen the whole place. "What do you guys think?"

"I'm fine with this," Shantanu agreed.

"It's all right, but we'll need to do a lot of work on the interiors. We need an ambience in which our creative juices can flow," Sachin said.

I looked at him with a strange expression.

"What?" he asked.

"Hey, the view from the balcony is really good," Sandeep called out.

We hadn't seen the place in much detail the previous time. We were on the tenth floor of the building. We went out to the balcony. The view from up there was indeed amazing. It reminded me of the heights that were awaiting us.

"This can be such a nice place to work. Can we make this one of the discussion rooms?" Sachin asked.

"Sure," I said, smiling.

"I can imagine us up here, in the middle of a serious discussion, and the white board being blown away by a strong wind," Shantanu said, as we all started laughing.

It was a very windy day.

"Let's move in soon. I can't wait to shift from the cramped-up place in my house. I need more space."

With some investment coming in, we had more options now. We were beginning to hire people. We needed a diverse team. We needed people who were interested in media, in society, in the Internet, technology and everything else.

We had also thought about the option of opening a TV channel when we made it big. But somewhere along the line we realized that it was not an effort that was worth it. We had enough eyeballs on the Internet, and we were dealing with a considerably different space.

Mr Ranjan also directed us to some other interesting incidents and stories. We still couldn't do too many at a time, but we were slowly doing more and more, as we began to get more people on board.

With momentum on our side, we opened up more avenues to people by launching many new features. One feature that became particularly popular was called twist. People could twist certain stories and add their own versions. Some people added funny twists to certain serious stories; some others twisted a sad story into something that was happy. It was interesting to see the twists and turns that people wished for. And that feature became a rage.

Also, people could now contribute directly on our website when they came across a needy story that moved them sufficiently. We were also looking at ways to expand our reach beyond urban India. The meeting of ideas, technology and people is such a wonderful and powerful thing.

With more hits came advertisement opportunities. Money was starting to flow in. With more money, came the confidence and ability to do more. The foundations were set.

But we had sworn to each other that however big we became, we would never compromise on one thing. We had had our debates and disagreements – my friends and I – but we had always agreed on one thing: we would never give up on our ideal of always doing the right thing.

We would never do something that we knew was not just, even if it meant that RS3 had to take a blow. We would always be aware of and abide by the right ethics. It was the one common thread that ran through all of us. The key word for us was "always".

Sometimes, people talk about being right and moral and ethical, only to make exceptions when it becomes inconvenient. We wanted to be different. Our morals were neither convenience-based unlike those of most people in society today, nor were they based on false foundations.

The journey we were about to embark on seemed like one of pure fun and fulfilment. There are perhaps many journeys we undertake in life, some of them even run parallel. We plan some of them, and some happen purely by accident. Life is an interesting mix of choice and chance, but I knew that even the chances that we get are converted into something big by the choices we make. The choice to be prepared, the choice to make use of those chances, the choice to do everything it takes.

It was all seemingly rosy, almost the dreamy life that I had imagined. But there was still a long way to go. It was just the beginning.

Chapter 10

One day, when I was in the midst of working on an interesting story, my phone buzzed. It was Megha. It had almost been a week since we had last met. I had just not had the time, even though she had always been in my thoughts. When we know that we have someone with us, we start taking them for granted. It's not like I had lost the enthusiasm to meet her; it's just that I knew that she was with me, and I didn't need to chase her constantly.

"Hello."

"Hi! Megha here."

“I recognize your voice.”

“Really?”

“Yes, of course.”

She laughed.

“How are you? I've not seen you for a few days.”

"I'm good. I gave you my number a week ago and you are calling now?"

"Well, I was just a bit busy with work.”

“Okay.”

“But even you didn't come to meet me."

"Yeah. I wanted to, but there were too many things happening."

"Okay.”

“Can we meet today?"

"Yes."

“Six?”

"Yeah."

"Okay, done."

"Bye."

"Bye."

And finally, I had her phone number!

Life at RS3 was moving along at breathtaking speed. But thankfully, we weren't running any race. We were just doing what we had to do, and were doing it at a good pace. I was working on a story featuring a young author and his latest work. We wanted to be the platform that provided deserving people with the opportunity to showcase their work.

Megha and I met that evening at S'adonner.

"You were supposed to take me on a drive, Mr Raghav," she said, kind of teasing me.

They somewhat confused me – those words of hers – for they were almost an indication that she had moved beyond reluctance. Yet her body language still had signs of resistance.

"Yeah sorry, got stuck with a few things. We'll go soon. I'm looking forward to it even more than you."

She looked straight into my eyes, the light that was born somewhere deep within her, showing on them.

"Why did you follow me from the cricket stadium that day?" she asked, after a pause. Somehow, she never wanted to let go of that question.

"I already answered that."

"When?"

"You want me to repeat it? You want to me to tell you once again that you were looking so pretty that I couldn't help but follow you?" I asked, smiling at her.

"Why not? I don't mind hearing praises. And you never said it directly."

"Actually, I also liked the way you talked."

"Really?"

"You want me to repeat that as well?"

She shook her head in a funny sort of way and smiled. It made her look cuter, and I kept looking at her.

"Which is your favourite cuisine?" she asked, breaking my stare.

"I like Chinese. You?"

"Nothing in particular, mostly anything Indian."

The group of people on the table next to ours were talking loudly. They seemed to be college students. We almost had to raise our voices to hear each other.

"Why did you agree to come with me for lunch that day? Do you go with any stranger who asks you out?" I asked, trying to be as loud as possible so that she could hear me and as mellow as possible so that nobody else could listen in to our conversation.

"What do you mean?"

"I mean..."

She interrupted me. "Even in the short time together, I had sensed that you have come to know me better than this. Maybe I was wrong."

"No..."

She interrupted me again. "I came with you because I saw a sincerity in your eyes; because I somehow felt a connect. We don't connect with everyone."

She hadn't taken that second question of mine too well.

"Sorry, that's not what I meant to ask. It was just... leave it."

"I would have got up and gone away if someone else had asked me such a question. I know that you didn't mean it that way, but please be more sensitive."

"Yes ma'am!"

"Damn," I thought. I had almost ruined it. I've learnt that one has to be very careful when saying anything to a girl. They manage to find something wrong in everything.

We fiddled around with our coffee cups for a while.

"Who's your best friend?" she asked.

"Best friend? Sachin. And yours?"

"Hmm.... I don't have a best friend as such."

"Why?"

"Don't know," she twisted her lips.

"You should find out."

"Actually, I did have such a friend, long ago, during the early days in school. But we lost touch. I guess best friends just happen to meet."

"Like we did."

"Hmm... I think there's still some way to go for that," she said, that little light reappearing in her eyes.

"We'll get there."

S'adonner was to become a usual, and so, a favourite meeting place. We not only talked about our lives, but also observed other people around us and talked about them. That was also in line with what I needed. The study of people, their behaviour and their stories is certainly one of the most interesting things in life. And somewhere along the line I understood that love is not only about seeing each other, it is also about looking at the world together.

Chapter 11

It was a pleasant Sunday morning, the sort of morning that is ideal for a lovely, long drive. The road was calm and almost without any traffic. Fresh, slightly chilling waves of wind blew into the car as we sped along on a wide road escorted by the trees that lined it. I looked at Megha. Her loosely hanging hair was fluttering in the wind and a few strands covered her face. I don't know how she managed it, but with every passing day she looked more and more beautiful. Of course, it was more a case of me falling deeper and deeper in love with her. The eye of love has the power to make anyone and anything seem pretty.

It had been more than two months since I had first met Megha. Finally, I had found the time to take her on a long-promised drive.

"Are you enjoying the drive, Megha?"

"Yeah." She smiled.

God, that smile of hers; it killed me.

I didn't quite know where that long winding road would lead us. I didn't know if it would ever end. But I somehow knew the path that Megha and I were on. All along, I constantly turned my head to look at her and saw that recognition in her eyes as well.

"Should we just go on or do you want to stop somewhere?" I asked, after we had travelled quite some distance.

"Can we turn into one of these small narrow roads?"

"Anything you say ma'am."

After a while, I turned left onto a side road. I had often thought of exploring those random narrow side roads that pass us by on the highway, but had never quite done it. We went on on that road for about fifteen minutes. It turned into a slightly muddy road, got narrower and narrower, and we arrived at a place where there was a small lake.

"Can we stop here?" Megha asked.

I stopped the car, and we got down. It would have made a good picnic spot, but there was no one around. One side of the road was filled with trees and it almost looked like a mini forest. On the other side was the lake, almost completely still. The far side of the lake had an even more dense population of trees, and we couldn't quite see what lay beyond them. The bridge that connected both banks looked somewhat old. It was pretty lowly built, and if the water were to rise four or five feet, it would seep onto the bridge. There were patches of grass growing all around. The place looked beautiful and inviting.

I looked at all the trees. In the right season, they would be full of flowers with some of them scattered across the bridge. It was a perfect place to relax. It was a perfect place to fall in love. I wondered how we had found such a beautiful place purely by chance.

We walked on the bridge. It looked a bit shaky, but was surprisingly quite sturdy. We stopped when we reached somewhere near the centre.

"What a lovely place," Megha said.

"Yes, lucky we came here."

The overcast sky, the slight chill in the air and occasional speedy bursts of wind only elevated the feeling of romance. We gazed away at the water and the trees, and into the sky. And perhaps it was there, on that bridge, that another bridge was built – the bridge between our hearts.

We came back to the bank and sat down on a bench. We had left home early and hadn't eaten breakfast. We opened some packed food we had brought along.

"Thanks for bringing me here. It feels so good," Megha said, as we were eating.

"Yes, it's amazing."

After we were done, we strolled around again, indulging in the atmosphere. I looked at Megha. We had grown very close now, yet, we had never even held hands. Perhaps it was that resistance of hers; it was still there inside her. As she walked beside me, I was compelled to put my hand out and touch hers. But somehow, I didn't.

"This place has a lot of charm. Even people who fight will make up. Couples who have started to hate each other will fall in love again," she said.

I loved it when she spoke such lines.

"How I wish that we were fighting or hated each other," I said.

She smiled at me.

"Do you think you can ever hate me?"

She was right; who could think of hating her? I shook my head, as she continued to smile.

"Why are you so silent? I know you are a romantic person. This is such a romantic place. Write me a poem, sing me a song, do something," she said, the tone tantalising and almost not her.

It was almost as if her heart had taken hold of her, replacing her thoughtful actions with a longing for romance. Love does that to us. We lose ourselves in the unending, almost extreme feeling of bliss, our senses collapsing into the swirl of emotions in our heart.

"Seems to me that you are the romantic."

She pushed at me slightly with her elbow.

"What makes you think that I can sing?" I asked.

"I heard you singing that day."

"Me? Where did you hear that? I can't sing for nuts."

"That's sad. You should learn."

I almost wondered if she had heard my heart sing.

We walked on, but suddenly her excitement somehow toned down. It was as if a switch was turned on (or turned off) somewhere, which pushed her to remain alert.

I kicked myself. "What a waste of an opportunity," I thought. I couldn't think of anything that I could do to impress her. I couldn't immediately conjure up any romantic words to make a poem. I wondered if I should just propose to her. That was all I could think of.

"What if I say that I feel like staying here with you forever?" I asked, trying to redeem myself.

"Really?"

"Yeah, why not?"

"Wow! That's such a nice thought. But I'll have to think about it."

"Huh?" I looked at her and frowned.

She smiled and pinched my cheek. That was the first time she had touched me.

"My, you look so cute," she said, as we stopped.

"Switch changed state again?" I thought.

"Anyway, this place and this day will always be in our hearts," I said.

"We should come here often."

"Yeah."

"Megha, can I hold your hand?" I said, after a few silent moments, almost putting my hands over my lips, trying to stop myself.

"Huh?"

"Sorry, I couldn't stop myself from asking."

She smiled a wider than usual smile and turned fully towards me. She stared at me for a while, her smile still on. And then, slowly, she held out both her hands. Somewhere in the second or two that it took for her to stretch those hands towards me, I saw streaks of opposition in her eyes. Why do some people contemplate so much? Why do they have to deliberate on something as natural and as inevitable as love? Perhaps I did find some answers later on in my life; yet I've never been able to validate such resistance.

I reached out and held her hands. My heart fluttered. It was as if all our feelings poured out of our bodies, flowed through our hands and filled us. I was impelled to pull her into my arms, but I resisted that impulse.

Just as I had begun to feel that the boundaries were beginning to melt, she pulled her arms back, slowly. We settled down on the bench once again. We spoke a lot that day, more than we had ever spoken before, not just in words that perhaps meant a lot, but also in silence.

We spoke through our eyes. We spoke in those numerous nuances that characterize the untold joy of first love.

I knew that day that my feelings towards her were more than simple attraction. It had to be deeper than that. It was somewhere there, sitting amongst nature, on the banks of that lake, that the line between attraction and love was crossed.

And that realization is such a wonderful feeling. Love. A burning flame that fans your heart. Something strange that just envelopes you, a feeling that almost drowns you. A heaviness that fills you, and a lightness that cannot keep you on the ground. That moment, when your eyes first meet, when the first rays from those eyes touch your soul, when the first brushes of love tantalisingly paint your senses. And you know in an instant!

For notes previously unheard of are played on, untouched chords are touched with a touch so endearing, and the strings of your heart are tugged at with a force never known before. You are just blown away. Your beating heart goes on, like the endless ocean, like the never ending road. Sometimes we become so immersed in love, that we even forget when this began; we begin to feel that there is no beginning or end to this, and that this love was always there.

The clouds in the sky did not shower us with any rain that day, but it was compensated for by the rain of love in our hearts.

Chapter 12

The frenzied emotions and highs of that drive date with Megha drove me into a state of reverie, my concentration ruined by the endless sparks and drowned in the river of affection. Time had come to tell her what I had not told her yet, and I somehow knew that she was waiting for it. Meanwhile on the work front, even through the valleys of my concentration, we were making good progress. We had planned a technology plus social conference in an engineering college. We had also invited a few other institutes to take part. Our endeavour was to achieve the dual purpose of providing an engaging and learning experience for students as well as taking RS3 to more young people. There were going to be technology sessions, workshops, discussions on social issues and much more. We had also managed to find a few prominent speakers from relevant domains.

We were truly excited. It was an important step for us. It was necessary to project ourselves in the right way to create an impact. With the successful organization of the conference we could potentially cross another stage, reach another level.

It was a big exercise to get everything together for such a conference. The logistics were a headache. Outsourcing to any random event management firm was ruled out as we wanted to bring an RS3 touch to it, which could only have been done when we were involved completely.

It was a three day event and even half way through it there was evidence of the raging impact that it eventually created. Student participation and reactions were exceptional. Talks by expert speakers were well received. Of course, the technology workshops were a hit, but even some of the discussions on social topics got an outstanding response. It was clear that people – even young people – were willing to support and participate in important social activities if they were made aware of the space and were pushed and empowered.

It became such a success, both directly – reflected by the reactions – and indirectly – reflected in the substantial increase in traffic to our website – that we decided to organize such conferences periodically.

There were a lot of interesting anecdotes and discussions during that conference that I'm sure will make an interesting read. They spawned some engrossing thoughts in me and somewhere along the line helped shape the future of RS3.

But I'll refrain from going into those. Because this story – this small, yet long story – is not about that. Maybe it's not even so much about RS3. It's about Megha and me. It's about love and all the complexity that it brings into our life.

The conference denied Megha and me the chance to meet each other for over four days, and we caught up every day the week after that to make up for the few days away from each other. And my work somewhat suffered; I could sense it. But somehow, Megha was even more important to me now.

One afternoon, when we were sitting in our usual meeting place at S'adonner, Sachin called me.

"Raghav, the story about that new invention in a village that is scheduled to be published today is not complete. Were you doing some work on it?"

"Oh yeah. Sorry, I'll come to office in about an hour."

"Okay, come quickly."

"What happened?" Megha asked, placing her hand over my mine, after we had hung up. Lately, her mannerisms and touches had significantly slashed the confusion in me. If she hadn't yet crossed the line, she was at least very close to it.

"Nothing, some work left incomplete. I'll do it later in the evening."

"No, you must go now. You shouldn't ignore your work," she said, concerned.

"I don't feel like leaving you now."

She smiled. "Raghav, we can meet again after you are done. Please go."

I reluctantly parted from her and went back to office. It was the beginning of getting pulled and sometimes pushed both ways: Megha and work, work and Megha.

I was lost in some self-discussion on the story I was working on, when Shantanu and Sandeep came to my desk. It was Sachin's birthday the next day. We were planning to throw a surprise party. It had been a long time since we had partied. We had not even celebrated our initial success yet. It is important to work hard and achieve something in life, but it is perhaps even more important to celebrate your success. What else is life, but a festival, a celebration?

"All set?" I asked.

"Yes. We've booked the hall, and everything else is in place. You were supposed to order the cake."

"Ah! I completely forgot. I'll do it today."

"What? You forgot? Do it before you forget again."

"Yeah, don't worry. I will. Have you informed Sachin's parents?"

"Yes, all taken care of."

We had invited some of our close friends and relatives. I had deliberated for a while on whether I should invite Megha to the party. I called her after Sandeep and Shantanu had left.

"Hey!"

"Hi Megha."

"What's going on? Were you dreaming about me?"

I laughed.

"Yeah, that's all I do day and night!" I said.

"You don't have to dream so much, I'm your reality."

"Yes, I know."

"You know?"

"By the way, tomorrow is Sachin's birthday. We are throwing a party. You must come."

"Yeah, I will."

"I'll pick you up from your office at five. Is that okay?"

"Yes."

I had talked a lot about my friends and partners to her, so she was also keen to meet them. I left the phone on my desk and went out into the balcony to feel the fresh evening air. After a while, Sachin came to the balcony holding my phone.

"Raghav, who's Megha?"

I was surprised, maybe somewhat tensed, to hear him utter her name. I suddenly realized that she was calling and he had seen her name flashing on my phone screen. I grabbed the phone from him and picked up the call.

"Yeah Megha, tell me."

"Just wanted to check if you were still dreaming about me."

With Sachin standing there, I couldn't utter any romantic lines.

"Yes."

"Just yes?"

"What about you?"

"Me? I'll tell you when we meet."

"I am waiting to hear."

"Hey, someone else is calling; I'll talk to you later."

"Okay, bye."

"Who is Megha?" Sachin queried again.

"A college friend."

"College friend? Strange. You never mentioned anything about her."

"She calls once in a while."

"I get the feeling that there's something going on. You are not in office so often these days. You meet her every day?"

"No, nothing of that sort is happening. You are just assuming..."

"C'mon, whom are you trying to lie to?" he interrupted me.

"Well... actually..."

And caught in the net of persuasiveness of my best friend, I had to reveal the truth. After I did, he dragged me inside, called Shantanu and Sandeep into a room and made a grand announcement. I had no option but to tell them everything. And it felt good to narrate that story, starting with the cricket match, the chance meeting, the chase, the wait, the dates, the drive and what not.

"Wow," they said in unison.

"Pretty filmy stuff!" Sachin remarked.

"Why didn't you tell us earlier?" Shantanu asked.

I wondered why I had hidden it from them; I was not sure. There was no reason for it. Sometimes we hide things from people closest to us for no reason at all.

"I was about to tell you guys."

"Ah, why do you hide such interesting things from us?"

"Anyway, it's good."

"Why don't you invite her tomorrow...?" Shantanu said, just as Sachin and Sandeep were leaving the room.

I had to stop him before he said something more and gave away our plans. Sachin heard him and stopped.

"Invite? For what?" he asked.

"Nothing, I was just telling him to invite her over to see our office," Shantanu redeemed himself, thankfully.

"I've already invited her," I whispered to him.

Even though the main reason for the party was Sachin's birthday, it was much more than that. That party was to be a celebration of our small, yet significant success. It was to be a celebration of our friendship, our values. And for me, it was also a celebration of my relationship with Megha.

Chapter 13

It was pitch dark. Everything was perfectly still. It was almost suffocating. We were all in the party hall, waiting for the surprise to begin. As the door opened and Sachin entered the hall, his parents following him, the lights came on and all those balloons hanging overhead burst open with a thousand sparkling little things falling all over him and around us. Does it sound pretty clichéd? It does, I know. But that's what it was. And it was like one of those turning points in life where darkness and silence are suddenly – in one lightning moment – replaced by light and celebration.

The words of probably the-most-sung song in history – happy birthday to you – filled the air, accompanied by the tremendous melody of the piano, leaving Sachin almost in tears of joy. I'm sure it's a great feeling when you get a pleasant surprise, when someone cares enough to do so.

He took small steps towards the main arena where a huge chocolate cake awaited him. The place was filled with music once again as he slashed the knife through the soft melting layers of the cake. We smeared it all over his face and he hugged each one of us.

"Thank you guys," he said, turning to the three of us standing together, after he had looked around. "This feeling is so special. It's the best day of my life so far. More than my birthday, this is a celebration of our success. Thank you so much," he continued, as everyone else clapped.

As the party gathered momentum, we all bonded with each other forming groups of our own, as Sachin moved around. I saw Megha standing alone and walked towards her. I had already introduced her to Shantanu and Sandeep. I called out to Sachin.

"Sachin, this is Megha. Megha, Sachin, my best friend," I said, as I pointed my hand towards both of them.

"Hello Megha."

"Hi Sachin, happy birthday." She gave him a big bouquet.

"Thank you."

Shantanu, playing the DJ of the night, turned on the music as some of us made our way towards the dance floor. Some of the less social ones just stood aside, as the dancing began. We lost ourselves in the beats of the music and the trance of our bodies. Everyone was pepped up and having fun. If it was a Bollywood movie, an item song could have perfectly fit in there.

The music only got louder and louder as the energy reached another level. It teased some of those lazy people looking on, enough to make them join us. Megha wasn't much of a party person and she stood a little distance away. Even though I signalled to her to join me, she hesitated. I didn't go and drag her, though I desperately wanted to, because my parents were watching. They didn't know about Megha, and though I knew that they wouldn't have a problem with my relationship with her, I still didn't want them to know that way.

After almost thirty minutes of high energy music and dance, the music turned light and romantic. It changed the mood completely, and I was hoping I could dance with Megha. All the others were still dancing away with somewhat lighter moves to suit the music. Megha though, still stood there just smiling. As another romantic track played out, our eyes met for an extended period of time.

Some people were already lapping up the sumptuous dinner. After more than an hour of crazy shaking of bodies, most of us were exhausted and hungry. Sachin and a few others were not yet in a mood to stop. I went over towards Megha, and we took dinner.

As we were eating – the food was excellent – something came over me, and I pulled Megha towards my parents and introduced her as a friend from college; I didn't tell them anything more. The music had turned loud once again and they almost couldn't hear anything anyway.

"Thank you for joining us on this day," a loud voice interrupted the flow of music. Sachin was speaking, standing in a corner, with a microphone in hand. He continued, "On this day of surprises and celebration. I'm glad that I was born this exact day, that year. Glad because somewhere that day, in the lines of my hand, and perhaps somewhere in the heavens, my destiny was written. The destiny that brought me to my friends and to this day, today. And I somehow know that if any of the four of us had stood here to speak today, we would have essentially said the same thing. I guess this is what dreams are made of. Maybe this is how special nights feel like. This is to friendship, to success, to all those people who have helped us along, those of you who are present here and those who aren't. This is to the life that has made this day so sweet. We know that your wishes are with us, for a grand future, for grander success. And I'm sure we will see all of you again, on another night, in another greater celebration."

The loud cheers that merged with the final few words of that unexpected speech almost drowned the emotions that all of us felt, and the party and the dancing resumed.

As the night raced along, people slowly began to leave the party even as the music continued. We decided to stay on well into the night, unwilling to let the euphoria die down. As the volume went up again, everyone joined in. Since his parents had left, Sachin called for a few drinks as he got to another high.

"Come on, let's dance," I begged Megha as she stood next to me.

"No, I don't dance very well."

"That's okay; nobody is going to see how well you dance. Just dance with me. Don't you want to?"

"Not in front of everyone here. We'll dance some other time."

I smiled and gave up.

"Why were you so hesitant to introduce me to your parents?" she asked.

"Don't know."

"Why are you thinking so much? You told me that your parents are very sweet and open-minded."

“Yeah, I know. Anyway you did meet them. But I had one confusion; I was thinking what I should say if they asked me who you are.”

She laughed. “You don't know?”

We looked at each other. We both knew it.

“Do you want to tell me something?” she queried.

“No nothing. Why? You want to say something?”

Even though I wanted to tell her right then, even though the words were almost on my lips, I controlled myself. I don't know why I hesitated. Was I afraid that she would say “no”? I don't think that was a possibility, but you never know what goes through a girl's mind, you just never know.

“God! Are you confused?” she asked.

“I've never been more sure.”

She seemed to like that. She moved closer to me – perhaps closer than she ever had – till her body was touching mine. I wanted to put my arms around her shoulder, but I resisted. As if she had sensed that, she held my hand without taking her eyes off me. After a few moments of longing, we both looked away towards the dance floor.

I looked at my friends celebrating. Being really happy is such a great feeling, but seeing your close friends happy is an even greater feeling.

We sat down, as all the others were still on the dance floor. That was a very happy day in my life. That night, the party almost never ended; it just went on and on and on. I silently wished that our progress and our success would also be never ending. I wished that we would have many more nights like that one.

There are a lot of good things in life, but celebrating success with your friends is something else. The sometimes loud, sometimes sober music of that eventful night, of that night of long ago, still goes on, somewhere in the hearts of the people who were party to that celebration. The smell of joy and zest that filled that night lingers ever on in our memories.

Chapter 14

The following evening – a somewhat calm Saturday evening – I sat in my room trying to write my first love letter. It was time to say those three words. This was a different scenario, because I already knew her answer. I could have just spoken to her, but I felt that a letter – a handwritten letter – would carry a deeper meaning. I wrote several pages of drafts and threw them away; I changed the words many times. But whatever words filled those pages, I knew that they would all have my true feelings in them. And that was enough.

Finally, I penned the last draft:

Dear Megha,

I somehow think and know that you've been waiting for this. I've been craving to tell you. These are words that have been born from the deepest part of my heart – from that part which is now full of you.

I Love You Megha. I love you for your ever enchanting smile. I love you for the way your eyes stare at me. I love you for the way they light up my life like nothing else can. I love you for the way you look when you are a little upset. I love you for those glances that pierce my heart and touch me inside at unknown depths. I love you for all the positive vibrations that you generate. I love you for everything that you are.

And of course I love you because you are the most beautiful girl I've ever seen and will ever see.

I know that I should have said this a long time ago, but I also know that we have spoken these words to each other many times, in numerous silent moments.

Forgive me if the chocolates have melted, for my heart itself has melted.

Love,
Raghav

I must have read through the letter a hundred times. Sometimes, I felt that those words were slightly over the top. Sometimes I felt that they were somewhat repetitive – I could have just written three words. At times, I felt that they were perhaps a little silly. But I let them be that way. I folded it neatly and put it in an envelope.

I felt so good. It was such a relief. Even though we had already felt our love for each other in the moments we had spent together, putting down my deepest feelings on paper was greatly satisfying. Whether happy or sad, our feelings need an outlet, and what better than sweet or bitter words put on paper to express them. Of course, no words could sufficiently articulate the deep love that I felt for her.

Chapter 15

The placid, quiet morning was a somewhat colourful contrast to the ruffling beats of my heart, as I stood outside Megha's door the next day. I didn't quite know how to act it out. I deliberated for a while, before placing the letter along with a bunch of red roses and a box of chocolates outside her door. My fingers, somewhat shaky with excitement, typed out a message requesting her to come out. I went some distance away and waited. I could still see the house clearly. As she opened the door, the sight of the roses and chocolates triggered off a smile on her face. I cannot even begin to sum up the uninhibited joy that swelled up inside me. Her eyes lingered on the letter for a few seconds. She looked up and saw me in the distance, her eyes fixed on me and her hands slowly opening the letter. She rolled her eyes down and began taking in the words that had poured out of my heart.

Throughout the time that she was reading the letter, the smile constantly graced her ever charming face. And then, she came out of the gate, ran towards me and hugged me. I wrapped my hands around her and held her tightly. That was the first time we had fallen into each other's arms.

The world around us disappeared into oblivion. It was as if there was darkness all around and we were the only light. The sugary touch of her soft body sent simmering strokes of heat all over me, as her fragrance filled the space around us and melted into the love that enveloped the air. It is unimaginable that someone can put that feeling into words that can equal the ecstasy that we felt.

"I love you," she said in an emotional voice.

Those words were like magic. There is nothing half so sweet in life as requited love. There is nothing half so sweet as hearing those three words from the love of your life. There is nothing half so sweet as a long embrace from your soul mate.

"I love you too."

"Why did you take so long to tell me?"

"I wanted to keep you waiting."

"Huh?"

"Didn't you enjoy this more because of the wait?"

She nodded and gave me another warm hug. We held each other for a while, and there was everything that I had ever wanted in life in that loving warm embrace from her.

We could feel the excitement. It was all over us. It was in the extra heartbeats, it was in the nervous touches, it was in the smile on our faces, which we could hardly control.

"Wow! I can't believe this feeling, I don't know what to do," she said.

I was completely lost for words. It was the most electrifying moment of my life. It felt like emotionally charged electrons were floating all over my body. It was a moment that I had forever waited for. It was something that I had longed to experience. Perhaps it is something that each one of us, somewhere deep within ourselves, wants to feel someday. There were hints of tears in our eyes.

"It's an incredible feeling. I cannot imagine anything better than this."

Our bodies were still clinging on to each other.

"You'll always be with me?" she asked, turning even more emotional, as we – almost reluctantly – let go of the embrace.

I nodded. "Yes."

"Forever? Whatever happens?" she asked again.

"Look into my eyes and you'll know."

She did, and from her expression I figured out that she saw the word promise written all over my eyes. And somewhere in that moment, lost in each other's eyes, we felt our souls melting into one another.

After I had managed to get my emotions under control, I looked around to see if anyone was watching us. After all, we were on the street in broad daylight. The light that had enveloped only the both of us slowly dispersed itself, as the world came back to light.

We decided to go shopping that day. I mean, she decided that we go shopping. I know that it wasn't a great decision from my point of view. If you take a girl shopping, it means – apart from breaching the limit on your credit card – endless waiting hours, as she tries out hundreds of dresses and footwear and bags and earrings and other random stuff. But I loved her, and people do stranger things in love. And all I wanted to do was to be with her.

"How do I look in this one?" she asked as she checked out a dress in a shopping centre.

"You look good in any dress."

"C'mon, tell me."

"Yes, this one looks good."

Even with my approval, she wasn't satisfied. She must have tried at least another ten before finalizing one. As the day went on, I felt as if I followed her into every shopping place in Bangalore.

"Did you enjoy shopping with me?" she asked, as we were in a restaurant in the evening.

"Yes."

"Really?"

"Of course."

"I know you guys don't enjoy shopping, especially when it goes on all day."

I laughed.

"That's true to some extent. But then if we have a beautiful girl for company, we don't mind it!"

I really did enjoy that shopping-day-out with her. I came to love everything about her: her mannerisms when she was picking a dress or trying out footwear, the way she asked me how she looked in a particular dress, the way she held my hand as we walked around.

And so our love story went one step further. It had indeed been an unbelievable journey so far. It just got better with time. I could not have hoped for a better person to be in love with.

In the coming days, we went to almost every place in town. We went for many drives together. We always enjoyed a drive, especially to that place near the lake. It became our new favourite place. We sometimes spent whole days there.

As I lay in bed one night, I reflected on my life so far. It was on a high; it had been for some time now. And I wondered if there was a low around the corner. Life is unpredictable. You never know when you suddenly find an almost un-negotiable curve. It never is a completely straight ride. And that worried me somewhat.

I wondered how I would react if something went wrong. What if our company hit a roadblock? What if I lost Megha? I couldn't even imagine that. I couldn't imagine life without her. It's strange that when we are struggling, we worry if we will ever get over that phase; we worry about not finding happiness. And when life becomes better, and we start experiencing joy and happiness, we worry that we may lose them.

I wasn't sure why those unwanted negative thoughts filled me. Was it just my mind playing tricks on me? Or was it a harbinger of some deep melancholy? With such thoughts floating inside me, I hardly slept that night.

Chapter 16

"I hope you're not neglecting your work," Megha said, as strawberry ice cream overflowed from her mouth.

We were sitting in an ice cream parlour.

"Don't worry about that, I'm doing okay."

"No, you shouldn't be doing just okay; you should be doing better than that."

"Yeah. I'll keep that in mind ma'am."

"Okay. Strawberry ice cream is nice, do you want some?" she asked, as she picked up a spoonful and thrust it towards my mouth. I couldn't refuse or resist a bite from her cup.

"Hmmm... yeah it's good."

"But you said you don't like strawberry flavour."

"Yeah, I don't like it. When did I say that the ice cream was good?"

"What?" she gave me a confused, yet knowledgeable look.

I started laughing, as she took another bite from her spoon.

"Can I get another spoon?" I asked.

"No!"

"Please?"

"It's over," she said, as she tilted her empty cup towards me.

"Sad," I said, disappointed. "Do you want one more scoop?"

"No, I've already eaten too much today."

"It's okay, you won't grow fat."

"Am I thin?" she asked.

The truth is, she wasn't thin, though she wasn't bulky either. But I couldn't tell her directly.

"Yeah, sort of."

"What do you mean by sort of?"

"I mean, you are of the right size. Why do you want to be thinner?"

She smiled that one-in-a-million smile. We held hands, as we made our way out of the parlour and walked towards her house. It was a fine, clear night. We passed roadside vendors who were about to pack-up. Small restaurants and chaat stalls were still busy, with people enjoying their Friday night.

"Sometimes the night frightens me," she said, as we walked past a closed jewellery shop.

"Why?"

"I don't know. I'm sort of scared of darkness. Maybe because I'm afraid that there will never be light again."

"You're afraid of darkness even when you are with me?"

She looked at me and slowly shook her head.

"Actually, the day scares me more than night," I said. "Who knows when the light of day will be gone? It's a strange reason to be afraid of the day, but at least the night makes us accept the darkness; the day sometimes gives us a false sense of hope."

We crossed the busy street and came to a calm stretch, and I thought about the busy and calm phases of our life. Which of them is better is debatable, but perhaps both are necessary.

Some people were in a hurry to go home; some people were strolling along slowly, maybe even thoughtfully. It occurred to me that though every one of us was here on this earth, each heart lives in its own world. Each heart lives in a bounded circle of its own – a circle that encompasses its own joys and sorrows, perhaps very different from other circles. Yet all circles are somewhere the same. It is interesting how we diverge, but somehow converge.

"Are we talking too much philosophy these days?" she asked.

"I heard somewhere that loves turns us into philosophers."

"Specially the thought of losing it."

"Megha, stop talking about losing love, we'll always be together," I assured her.

"I hope so."

"We will," I assured her again.

Her bright face shone in the darkness of the night. She was wearing a black woollen jersey over her salwar, and it seemed to enhance the warmth that she generated. It almost made me feel warmer. She adjusted her dupatta often, as the breeze grew stronger. Even though she wasn't smiling, her face still had marks of those countless smiles that she had smiled.

We passed a small tea stall from which an old Hindi song could be heard:

Lag ja gale ke phir
Ye hasin raat ho na ho
Shaayad phir is janam mein
Mulaaqaat ho na ho
Lag jaa gale se ...

(Fall into my arms
This beautiful a night may not come again
Perhaps in this birth
We may not meet again
Fall into my arms ...)

The words of the song reverberated in my ears, as the music travelled across the street and perhaps into the hearts of people.

My attention turned to the warm chill of Megha's hands in mine. I clutched them a little more firmly. She looked at me, that smile reappearing on her face.

We didn't speak too much during the walk that night. Sometimes words don't mean anything. Words are not even enough to express our deepest feelings. What could be more satisfying than hearing words that are unsaid? What is more fulfilling than the silent communion of hearts?

We were so lost in the somewhat dark reverie of the almost undisturbed night and didn't even realize that we had reached her house. We sunk into each other's arms and parted after a longer than usual embrace.

Those were memorable days, days that will forever bring a smile to my face, days that serve as reminders of how beautiful life can be.

Chapter 17

The next few weeks were like a breeze – a slow moving, endless breeze – which carried the fragrance of love to every corner of our souls.

Megha called me one afternoon. I was at my desk in office, immersed in something.

"I need to go to Pune. My dad is not well."

"What happened?"

"Not really sure. He's in the hospital."

"Shall I come with you?"

"No no, I'll manage. I'm already on my way to the airport."

"Okay, call me if you need anything."

"Yes, bye."

"Take care."

I silently prayed for her dad.

I was sifting through some of our recent stories. The various, some hilarious, some particularly serious responses we had got were more than interesting; and somewhere along the line, I felt that each of them contained within, an untold deeper meaning. It was important feedback, one that gave us some sense of the direction that we needed to take.

One story, which was on reservation in higher education, was very popular. We had included every possible minute detail, almost every possible statistic. Division on the basis of anything interests us Indians no end. I scanned through the comments, and as expected, everyone was divided in their opinion.

I made a note of my observations and comments. Since we now had more people, we could do more stories. When we started initially, we could hardly do one or two significant ones in a week. I also looked at some of the requests we had got from various people to publish their stories on our main page. As I was surfing through them, Mr Ranjan called me. It had been some time since we had spoken, and he desired to talk to me about something. I agreed to visit him the next evening.

I remembered his first interview with us. That story had been a decent success. There had also been some investigation into the scandal because of the story, and it was still on. But we hadn't really followed up too much after having put out all phases of that story, though some people continued to post updates occasionally.

Our role was to take the stories to the people. Our role was dissemination of the right information to as many people as possible. Whether a story achieved its ultimate objective was really up to the people themselves, or maybe up to activists like Mr Ranjan.

Knowing your role clearly is one of the most vital things in life. One can't do everything. Everyone has to play his or her role for things to fall in place. It was part of the reason why we were making good progress and were in the right direction. We knew our role in the scheme of things, and we tried to play it as well as we could.

Sachin came to my desk. We had to prepare a presentation for Mr Simon. He periodically visited us to see how we were progressing. He scanned through our ideas and future plans and helped us tune our roadmap. His guidance played a big part in our success, because even though we were doing well and had great ideas, his experience was crucial in guarding us from going off the track.

We discussed the progress we had made over the last few weeks as well as our strategies. We looked at some numbers and statistics. Once we had the entire material ready, Sachin went back to his desk to prepare the presentation.

I tried to call Megha, but couldn't reach her. She called me late that night. It was the first time that I had noticed a sorrow in her voice.

"Hi, how's your dad now?"

"He's okay, but still not feeling too good," she said.

"What are the doctors saying, anything real serious?"

"He was feeling very weak and couldn't even eat properly. He's probably all right now."

"Thank God. Don't worry too much, things will be fine."

"Yeah."

"Who's there with you?"

"No one right now. I didn't want my mother to stay here all night."

"You're going to be in the hospital all night?"

"Ummm."

"I should have come with you."

"No, that's okay. Anyway I can call you whenever I feel like talking to you."

We spoke for more than a few minutes. I did my best to make her feel better and her voice was considerably more assured when we hung up.

And perhaps, another line was crossed. Sharing happy moments with the person you love is one thing, but sharing a sober moment is something totally different. It takes your relationship to a new level altogether.

Chapter 18

We were with Mr Simon in our office, running through the presentation. He gave us subtle hints as usual, and overall, he was satisfied with what he saw. We needed a bigger investment if we desired to grow faster. We had a more than decent money flow – perhaps enough to sustain at the current level – but we had to aim higher. Also, there was plenty to do, and we still didn't have enough resources. Mr Simon promised to recommend us to bigger investors.

"Raghav, look at these numbers," Sachin said, after Mr Simon had left. He had pulled out some usage statistics.

"Yeah?" I looked at his laptop screen.

"Do you think we are doing the right things? I hope we are not building useless features and harming the current ones."

"Well, I'm sure they are not useless, but yeah, the numbers are a little bit worrying. And even the main stories haven't generated too much interested this week."

"Maybe people are a little tired of the same kind of stories. We need something different, maybe we need to venture into a totally different domain."

"Yeah."

"Send me this, I'll check."

"Just a sec," he said. He was receiving a call on his phone. "Hello..."

Just then, Shantanu called out to me. I went out of the room. There was a slightly short, thin, middle-aged man, standing next to him.

"Raghav, he's Mr Dixit. He wants to talk to us about a potential advertisement."

"Hello Mr Dixit, please come."

We shook hands and I took him into a discussion room.

"Tell me."

"I'm the secretary of Mr Dhruv Kumar."

"Dhruv Kumar?"

"He's a prominent and powerful MLA here."

"Okay, yeah I've heard of him."

"The next general elections are approaching and we are looking at advertisement options."

"You want to run an advertising campaign for elections on RS3?"

"Yes. We want to highlight all the good work Mr Dhruv has done for his constituency."

As far as I had heard, Mr Dhruv had done precious little good since being elected in the last election. I was almost about to say something to that effect, but I managed to stop myself.

"Why do you want to advertise on RS3?"

"A large number of visitors to your website are young people. This election can potentially be decided by their votes."

"Only if a significant percentage of them vote," I said, as if knowing how many young people actually vote. That perception was probably because I had never voted.

"That's what we want to change. And we want this to be more than an advertisement, we want it to bc like a story; one of your main stories."

"Hmmm... we don't usually do that."

"Is there is any reason you shouldn't now?"

I just looked at him and then looked down, lost in thought.

"Can I make a short presentation?" he asked.

"What's it about?"

"It's about Mr Dhruv and also a little bit about our party."

I was reluctant to take it further since I was sure that the advertisement would only be an eyewash, an attempt to hide the fact that they had done nothing for the good of the people. But I thought that it would do no harm to sit through his presentation.

"Okay." I nodded.

He opened his laptop and took some time before he was ready. He turned it sideways so that it was visible to me. The presentation and the material he showed were indeed impressive. If only everything it claimed was true and complete!

"We want the story to create a tremendous impact. We'll start with Mr Dhruv and then we'll slowly showcase the other prominent people, and of course the achievements of our party," he said, after he was done with the presentation.

"We have to think about it. We don't usually allow political advertisements."

"But why?"

I was trying to conjure up a polite reason.

"We've allocated a huge budget for ads this time. There is a lot of money to be made," he said.

We all seem to think that it doesn't quite matter who wins elections in India. All parties, all people in power, are the same. At least that's the popular opinion. Thinking along those lines, I was almost tempted to agree to his proposal. "If the ad eventually doesn't affect anything, then why should we worry?" I thought.

But I nipped those thoughts in the bud, knowing fully well that whatever the impact, it was completely against our basic values.

"Sorry, I don't think we'll publish such ads."

"You can think about it sir. Maybe I can come back tomorrow."

"No, I don't think we'll change our mind on this."

"But sir..."

I cut him off. He insisted that he would check with me again, sometime later. And he did. In fact Mr Dhruv himself called our office trying to convince us, and offering more than expected amounts of money. We didn't have anything to say. We didn't tolerate anything distorted or fraudulent in RS3. Those considerations were on top of our priority list, and we sincerely hoped that we would always maintain our clean slate.

That episode, though it doesn't seem too significant on the surface, brought out some very positive things. It pressed home the point that we at RS3 didn't give in to anything – whoever or whatever it was – that didn't match up to our principles. It also showed that RS3 was indeed starting to reach good levels of popularity, at least among the youth, enough for even political parties to think about advertising with us.

But perhaps, the most important of them all was that it made me rethink my indifference to the most important aspect of democracy. Who is to say that every person who comes to power will not make a positive impact? Who is to say that every vote doesn't make a difference? I decided that the next general elections would have the privilege of counting my vote!

It's surprising how many hidden positives we can discover beyond the outwardly visible portions of a seemingly insignificant event in our lives.

Chapter 19

The constant context switch between Megha and RS3, between love and passion, filled up every second of my days, and left my mind with almost no free cycles. Megha was back after spending a week in Pune. Her dad was much better now and was back home. It felt like we hadn't seen each other for ages.

We drove to our favourite place near the lake. The enchantment of that place could almost turn any feeling of glum into a strange inner joy. We were talking about her dad's condition.

"He has multiple problems. He's had a history of illness and now there are other complications. He's very weak."

"Don't worry, he'll be okay."

"Sometimes I wish that I was in Pune and could spend more time with him. He has worked so hard to take good care of me all these years, and I can't be near him at this time."

Though she had a good point there, I felt a pinch in my heart. I silently thought, "What about us?" Of course that was not the time for those thoughts. If her dad needed her, she had to be there for him.

"Why did you come to Bangalore after your graduation? You could've found a job there?"

"It's easier here. There are more options."

"Yeah. It's strange, we've not discussed too much about our families," I said.

"Yes, we've been immersed in ourselves."

"You know about my family, there's not much more to say as such."

"Yeah."

"Who else is there in your family? You said you have a sister."

"Yeah."

"Younger?"

"No, elder."

"What does she do?" I asked.

"She was never too interested in mainstream stuff. My parents tried to persuade her to be an engineer, but she was more keen on art. So she's not really doing anything as such. She's good at painting, so she sometimes spends time on that. But she's a little crazy and nobody understands her. She married about a year ago. I don't know how her husband tolerates her." She shook her head.

"That's nice."

"What? It's nice that my sister is crazy?"

"No, I mean it's nice that she didn't listen to your parents; I've got tired of meeting only engineers."

"What? Then it's sad that you met me. You should have met some artist."

"You are right, my bad luck!"

She touched my forehead with her pointer finger and pushed me, as we both laughed.

We didn't talk about anything for quite some time after that. We stood on the bridge, the heavenly silence of the somewhat soft afternoon making the sound of the waves in our hearts almost vividly audible. The trees were blooming with colourful flowers; it was the beginning of spring. The lake embodied the silence of the place.
It was a great place to live your melancholy or happiness. It was a beautiful place to experience solitude or togetherness.

Megha rested her head on my shoulders, and I held her with one arm. I had spent a lot of silent moments with her, but somehow, the silence that day was scary; the calm was overwhelming. I wondered if a thundering storm was about to unleash itself.

That day, we walked further than we usually did. We walked well past the end of the lake; we walked past some empty fields, until we could spot a few small houses and huts in the distance, probably part of a farm. We turned back after a while.

True to my thoughts, the heavens opened up, and the cold drops of rain gently caressed our bodies, somewhat spluttering the waters of our hearts. The trees now began to look fresher and greener as if the waters had quenched their thirst, much like love had quenched the thirst of our souls. The flowers strewn all around, almost dead, seemed to come alive, their colours now bright and radiant, much like those smiles that emanate from the beautiful people in our lives.

Slowly, it got heavier and heavier, and there were already tiny ponds forming all around us. We didn't have anywhere to run for cover, except inside the car – it was now too heavy for any tree to shield us. I tried to drag Megha towards the car, but she pulled me back.

"Let's get drenched."

"What?"

"Yes, I love getting wet in the rain. It's been such a long time."

I obliged. Why would I refuse? There I was, standing in the rain, in such a romantic place, with the girl I loved. I sometimes wonder what love and romance would be without music and rain. What would life itself be without them?

"It's so cold na," she said.

"Yeah, we'll end up falling ill."

"That's okay, it's good to fall ill once in a while."

"Why is that?"

"Don't know," she shrugged her shoulders.

"Is it also good to experience sorrow sometimes?"

"Oh God, now don't turn this into a philosophical discussion on happiness and sorrow," she laughed.

She looked stunning in the rain, in her wet clothes. The water all over her face and lips made her even more attractive. The unending warmth that radiated from her cold body heightened the waves within me, like the high tide of the ocean on a full moon night.

"You're looking so beautiful today."

"Ummm... don't I look beautiful on other days?" she asked, with a kind of puzzled smile on her face.

"You do, but today you are mesmerising me. Maybe it's the rain," I said, as I held her.

"Raghav sir, control yourself; this is a public place."

"Yeah? There's no one here."

She pushed at me and ran away. That was such a wonderful moment – that moment in the rain with Megha. I could almost hear a grand piece of music playing out. It was as if the notes of that melody rose high up into the air and touched the heavens above. It was almost filmy. It was like one of those dreamy sequences in a romantic, feel good Bollywood movie.

And it poured and poured and poured that day. Endless rain. Endless emotions. Endless romance. Endless love.

Chapter 20

We were in a discussion in our office one night – all four of us. We had got the sense that RS3 was stagnating. We still had a healthy number of visitors. We still had what we thought were quality stories and content. But none of our new ideas were truly working. We were not attracting too many new people. We hadn't had a "hit" story for quite some time.

"Raghav, we need to do something. Something different, maybe something new," Sachin remarked.

"Yes, I think all of us realize that we haven't done enough in the last few weeks. I mean, we haven't grown," I responded.

"Yeah. Sandeep and I are working to make sure that we have the technology base to scale and support whatever we need to," Shantanu chipped in. "Maybe we can quickly bring in one of the new features we were planning. Might help."

We looked at our roadmap. There were thoughts of changing our priorities. But one thing was clear; we needed fresh content. It was content that drove our website. No number of new features would help if we did not have great stories.

The discussion continued for a long time, well into the night. We didn't hit the panic button, it wasn't that bad. But when you don't make continuous progress, there definitely is some cause for worry.

Of course my time was being divided between Megha and work. I still spent quite a big part of my day at work. But it's not about the amount of time you spend. It never is. It's always about the quality of work. Some conversation with her, or some moment we had spent together, or if nothing else, just her smile, was always in my thoughts and that did take a toll on my work.

I knew that Megha was an inseparable part of my life, but I needed to be able to concentrate purely on RS3 at least when I was in office. That was one thing I was bad at. It was admittedly a dangerous weakness. Before Megha came into my life, I hadn't had too many distractions, and so I had been able to do what was required, with concentration.

I am not suggesting that Megha was a distraction; she surely wasn't. At least she should not have been. Love should never be a distraction. On the contrary, we should know that it has the ability to be the inspiration to work harder.

I resolved to balance my time better. I resolved to concentrate on one thing at a time. I owed at least this much to my friends.

"Sorry, I've been a little bit lazy lately. I need to pick myself up," I said to Sachin, as I sat next to him.

"Happens, we all have our periods of ups and downs. And really, this can't just be about one or two of us being a little lax. If it is, then it means that our foundations are shaky," Sachin said.

He was right. No organization can depend on the performance of a few individuals. We had to reach a point where it didn't matter significantly even when a couple of us couldn't give our best for a few days.

"Yes."

We had to reinvent ourselves; we had to do something more. Every organization does experience such a phase, but we felt that it was too early for us to be going through this. Sometimes we felt that we were overreacting, but you can't ignore your instinctive feelings.

There were raging arguments amongst us, most of them inconclusive even after hours of debate. Needless to say there were strong disagreements as well, but it didn't affect our resolve to always be together. It was not about individual egos, it was about the team winning.

"Why don't you ask Megha to join us?"

I was about to leave office to meet her, when Sachin put this question to me.

"Yeah, I've been thinking about that actually. I'm going to meet her now, I'll ask her."

I made my way out, down the stairs and walked the slightly long distance to her office. It was a beautiful evening. The sun must have still been somewhat visible, somewhere beyond the horizon. The colourful streaks of natural paint that spread far and wide across the endless sky were like the different hues that characterize our lives.

I waited at the gates of her office building, for the... well, I'd lost count. It was a few minutes before I saw her walking down the path leading towards the gate. She walked past the gate and came towards me.

"Sorry, I'm late. Some important work cropped up," she said.

"It's okay."

"I have to get back to work in an hour."

"Okay, do you want to go somewhere or...?" I asked.

"Can we have something on the roadside?"

"On the roadside?"

"Yeah."

"Those roadside stalls are really unclean. We can go to the nearby restaurant," I said.

"Come on, you always say this. They are sufficiently clean and the taste is better than those big restaurants. Let's go please."

"Okay." I wondered if a boy had ever won an argument with the girl he loved.

We walked towards one of the roadside chaat stalls, where she ordered a couple of dishes.

"What do you want?" she asked.

"Nothing, I'm not feeling hungry."

"You don't have to be hungry to eat this," she said, making a face.

I just shook my head, as she took the plate from the stall vendor. She started enjoying the food, as I looked at her and derived a pleasure from watching her eat. She tried to force me to eat some of it, and I refused.

"You have to eat it." She pushed the spoon into my mouth. She laughed looking my face.

"Megha, my friends were asking whether you would like to join us," I said, as she ordered more.

"Huh?"

"Do you want to join RS3?"

"RS3? Me? But I'm not very good at anything. I don't know how I'm managing this job here."

She never bragged about herself. That was one of the many qualities about her that I found attractive.

"Don't underestimate yourself. And anyway I'll be there; we'll find some way to help you along. It'll be nice to work together."

"Yeah. Okay, I'll think about it."

Someone called her, and she had to rush back to office.

"Sorry, I have to go. I'll see you tomorrow. Bye."

"Bye."

Back in my office, I was still thinking about Megha, when I remembered my resolution. So I choked those thoughts of her and did my best to get some work done. Yet, she was in my mind every other minute. I wondered how it would feel like to work with her, to have her near me all the time, to hear her voice more often.

Chapter 21

The moonless, starless, cloudy sky looked down upon me as if it were concealing something. Sometimes I wonder if we know the reality in life and yet pretend not to see it. The moon was very much there, somewhere beyond the clouds – much like the stars – and I knew it. Yet I saw only the clouds.

My watch showed fifty-five minutes past eleven. There were five minutes left for Megha's birthday on the sixth day of May. I had not seen her face for more than a week, due to various reasons. I stood at her doorstep, waiting for the clock to tick over.

Around a minute before midnight, I rang the doorbell. Three more rings and a couple of minutes later, Megha opened the door. She looked unbelievably attractive in her night dress, with her unkept hair falling all over her.

"Raghav!"

"Happy birthday, Megha," I said, as I presented her with flowers. Whatever you give or don't give to a girl, a bunch of flowers is a must.

"Thank you! I seriously didn't expect you to come here, I was only hoping for a call."

"May I come in ma'am," I said.

She hesitated for a bit, but couldn't refuse. "Of course!"

I had never gone inside her house before that. It was a small place, but looked spacious enough as it didn't have a lot of furniture.

"Isn't your friend at home?"

"No, she's out of town."

"Okay. And here's your gift." I placed the box of chocolate cake I was carrying, on a table nearby, and presented her with a gift.

"Thank you!"

"Don't you want to open it?" I asked.

She opened it, neatly removing the gift wrapping. She seemed to like what she saw.

"It's really nice, thank you Raghav."

"You like it?"

"Yes."

It was a cute, well-designed bracelet, somewhat overtly decorated with small rings. It wasn't a very expensive one, but I was glad that she liked it.

"I'm bad at choosing gifts. I was afraid that you may not like it."

"I must say that your choices are good," she said, as she wore it and watched it wrapped around her wrist.

"Now to the main thing: the cake."

I opened the box placed on the table. The lone candle that I had had been carefully placed, ready to be set alight in celebration of another year in her life.

"Wait, I'll get a knife," she said.

"No you sit here, I'll get it. Where can I find it?"

She pointed towards the kitchen. It took me a frustrating two minutes to find a knife.

"Did you find it?" she called out.

"Yes," I shouted, as I came back.

I handed it to her. I tried to light the candle. Three wasted, indifferent match sticks later, I found fire in one of them, enough for the candle to glow. It reminded me of the fire that had been kindled in my heart in the very first meeting with Megha, though it had taken me a few days to realize the depth of that rage.

"Here you go."

As the sweet breath of air that emanated from her lips blew out the candle and she cut the cake, I took a piece and put it in her mouth. She took a bite and fed the rest of the piece to me. We settled down there and talked for a few minutes. We relished those moments of togetherness.

"How old are you now?" I didn't really know her exact year of birth, though I had guessed it.

"Hmm... should I tell you?"

"Yeah, why not?"

"Twenty two."

"The day you were born must have been a wonderful day."

"How do you know?"

"I somehow know. Without the moment that brought you into this world, I would never have met you. I would never have known this feeling of love."

"Hmm... I don't know. Sometimes I feel that it would have been good if I had never been born at all."

"What? You wouldn't want to be born even to meet me?"

"Not like that, but sometimes life is just too complex."

"What's so complex about your life right now?"

She just shook her head in a weird, confusing sort of way.

"Now what is that supposed to mean?"

"I was just saying generally..."

With that, we fell into silence, the happiness of her birthday and the excitement within me, melting into the serene night, into a strange calm.

If you people, who are reading this, felt that it was a very mellow description of the celebration of Megha's first birthday with me, if you felt that somewhere, something was missing, you are right. Because I felt that too. There was no music. There was no dance. There were no hugs, no endearing glances from her. It almost didn't feel like a special occasion.

Something was certainly wrong. I felt that she wasn't completely happy. Yes, she enjoyed the small celebration with me, but the characteristic "wow" exclamations and laughs were absent. However much she tried to hide it, her meek smiles gave her away. Perhaps she also knew that I had recognized that, but I didn't speak to her about it. I didn't want to spoil the feeling on that special day. Maybe I saw those hidden signs and yet didn't see them, just like I didn't see the moon that night.

"Okay, I'll leave now. Will see you in the afternoon," I said, as I left her.

Chapter 22

"You seem to be a little down, that too on this day. What happened?" I asked Megha, as we were having lunch in a posh restaurant that afternoon, on her birthday. I had to ask her now.

"Nothing as such, just like that."

"C'mon Megha, it's your birthday today and you are looking sad. Please tell me, what's the matter?"

"No Raghav, I'm all right. You tell me, how's your company doing? You told me that you were trying to get more investment," she tried to cut out that topic of her mellowness.

"Yes, we are trying. Something should happen soon."

She usually placed her hand on mine on and off, but that day her hand was constantly touching mine; she didn't let it go. The faint feeling that something was amiss was now almost a certainty. We had become so close to each other that we could smell melancholy in the other's heart. We could even see the tears hidden behind.

When we were almost done with lunch, she took out something from her handbag. It was a gift-wrapped, box-like structure.

"This is for you."

"What's this?"

"It's a gift." she said.

"Gift? What gift? It's your birthday, not mine."

"You've given me so many gifts, haven't you? It's time I also gave you one." She tried to smile.

I was surprised and was about to open it, when she stopped me.

"You can open this after you go home, don't open it here."

"Why?"

"Please Raghav."

When the girl you love says "please", you don't have an option, do you? I had to accede to her order. I kept the box on the table.

"Take me on a drive," she said, after a pause.

"Sure," I said. I had the car with me that day.

Outside, the meeting of the somewhat warm afternoon and predictably cool evening infused a rather sedate feeling to the already feeble spirit that had characterized Megha's birthday. Yet perhaps, there was a strange strength in it.

We went on random roads; we just went where we felt like going. Sometimes I hope life could be like that. I hope the world gives us the chance to take whatever path we feel like taking. Perhaps we actually do have that chance. Perhaps we only make a choice to not take those paths.

"Megha, did you give some thought to joining RS3?" I asked as we were going along.

"Yeah, I've been thinking. Maybe it's not a bad idea. But give me a few days."

"Okay."

"Is it okay for us to work together? I mean, will you be able to concentrate with me in front of you the whole day?"

I laughed. "I'll try!"

"Then I better not join."

"Megha, I will concentrate, don't worry about that," I said.

She just looked at me.

"Okay, take a few days and let me know. Base it purely on whether you would like to work with us; don't worry about other things," I added.

She nodded. I could sense that she was certainly not completely herself that day. There was something bothering her, and I couldn't refrain myself from asked her again.

"Megha, are you okay? I really sense that something is wrong."

"No, I'm fine. What could be wrong with you in my life?" She smiled another mild smile.

If I had persisted, she might have shared it with me. But I have never been one to force people. It irritates me no end when people insist on something, and I would never want to inflict that pain on someone. I knew that she would tell me when she wanted to.

But when I look back, I have to acknowledge that it was a blunder to have taken a "no". I should have, by any means possible, dug out what was running through her. But I chose to let it be. I didn't know then that it was to be the worst choice I had ever made in my life. I didn't know then that the ghosts of that day and moment would forever haunt me.

Chapter 23

The afternoon had faded into memory and the evening had settled the fight between warm and cold, when I dropped her home.

"Love you," she said, as she hugged me.

"Love you," I responded.

She kept looking at me as she went into her house.

I stopped at a medical store on the way home, to pick up some medicines for my mom.

As I was walking up the stairs to my home, I remembered that I had forgotten Megha's gift in the car. I went back to retrieve it. I was anxious to open it. I shut the door of my room behind me, and hastily tore open the wrapper and opened the box. It was a beautiful silver coloured watch, with a big screen and metal straps that fit perfectly on my hand. It was really lovely, and I admired it for a while. There was also a letter. I eagerly unfolded the somewhat weak and simple folds. Even now, when I remember that moment, I sometimes wish that I could unfold the complexity of my life with such ease.

The words that filled the letter – very neatly written, with somewhat rough edges – were as follows:

Dear Raghav,

Thank you for the wonderful time together. These have been the best days of my life without any doubt. The way we met, the way you chased me, the way you have treated me. The numerous dates, the numerous long drives, the warmth, I have loved them all. Thank you for loving me so much. You are the best person I could have ever hoped to be with.

I also love you and will continue to do so forever. But I have been thinking lately, that this relationship is holding up our ability to do other things. I know for sure that you have lost focus on your work to some extent, and I don't want that to happen. You have immense potential to achieve great success, and I truly wish that you get there.

My dad is still unwell, and my family needs me to be with them. Also, I have a job offer in Pune. It will allow me to be with my family as well as give me a better pay check.

I think it's best for both of us to hold this relationship for a few years till we settle down in our career and handle other responsibilities we have. So, I've made a decision. It was very hard, but one that had to be made.

I'm leaving today. I'll meet you again this day, exactly after five years, and that's a promise. I also promise that I'll still love you. I promise that we will be back together. Also, if things go so well that I feel we can get back together sooner, I'll contact you.

I could have told this to you in person, but I know that you would have tried to convince me. It would have been impossible for me to leave you like that.

Five years is a really long time and it may seem unreasonable to you. I know that I don't have the right to take away five years of your life. If you don't agree with my decision, you are free to move on in life. I want you to know that I'm with you in whatever decision you take, and I fervently hope that you are with me in this decision of mine.

I am extremely sorry for this, but I feel that it is necessary. Only I know the pain I went through when I was writing this letter. I still love you and will be waiting for you exactly five years from now at our favourite place near the lake.

And thank you again, for making my birthday so special.

Lots of love,
Megha
(May 6, 2006)

I could hardly believe what I had just read. I scanned through it again as I picked up my cell phone and frantically dialled her number; but her phone was switched off.

I grabbed the car keys and ran out of my house. I drove faster than I had ever done. I reached her house and desperately pushed at the bell and knocked on the door many times. There was no response. It seemed as if there was no one at home. I asked the people next door, but nobody knew anything.

I didn't know what to do. "Where should I go now?" I thought. I knew that she would be going to Pune, but I wasn't sure if she was taking a bus or a flight. I had to try something.

The airport was at least an hour away. I could try to get to the bus stand in fifteen minutes. So I rushed there and searched all Pune-bound buses. I knew that she couldn't have left so soon, as I had dropped her off only about an hour back.

I had no luck. She was not to be found anywhere at the bus stand. I tried calling on her cell every five minutes, but it was always switched off. I decided to go to the airport.

It took me close to an hour and a half to get there. I did my best, I drove like crazy, and I even skipped a signal or two, whenever I could. But we can only drive as fast as the traffic allows us to. Something that often irritated me – the traffic – had to rear its ugly head even in this moment of anxiety and hurry. Such is life.

Getting to the airport was only the first step. I had forgotten that I would not be allowed to go inside without a ticket. I scanned the people standing outside, but there was no sign of Megha. Without another option, I went to one of the ticket counters outside and bought a ticket to Pune. Thankfully, I had my credit card with me. I had to go in.

I made my way inside and searched desperately. The book shop, the restaurants, the check-in counters, everywhere. I couldn't find her anywhere. I had to go further. I took my boarding pass and went through security check. I checked at every gate. Of course, I had to be careful. I couldn't run around randomly, since it was the airport.

Whatever I tried, I couldn't find her. I had only one option now: go to Pune. Since I already had bought a ticket, I decided to go the same day. I still kept looking for her.

Finally, I sat down at the gate from which my flight was to depart. I was praying silently. I hoped that I would somehow meet Megha. I knew that if I met her soon, I could convince her to reverse her decision. There are always alternate solutions to every problem in life.

I called my dad and tried to sound as normal as I could.

"Hello."

"Hello dad, I have to go to Pune urgently for a business meeting. I'll be leaving tonight directly from office. I think it may be a day or two before I return."

"Okay, don't you want to at least come home and take some of your clothes?"

"That's all right dad, I may not have the time to come home now. And I'm going to leave your car parked at the airport. Sorry about that."

"That's okay, you take care. Call me once you get there."

"Sure dad, bye."

It was half past nine; the flight was still one hour away. In the rush to find her, the reality had not even crept into me. My heart still couldn't believe what had transpired in the last few hours.

Slowly, the gravity of the situation began to dawn on me. The potential that it had, to tear my life into pieces, unnerved me. I had often thought about how it would feel if I ever had to part from Megha. I had not even been able to fathom that pain. I had not been able to bear it even in my imagination. And now, that situation was scarily close to being a reality.

I closed my eyes. It was too heavy for me to handle. The hope that I would find her soon, kept the tears from coming out, but internally, I was bleeding. My world collapsed. I felt my head turning. All the running around didn't help the cause. I didn't know what was happening. I fainted.

Chapter 24

The cool breeze that entered through the window and brought in the sweetness of the day outside woke me up next morning. I was at home, and even those sweet, mini waves of the breeze only managed to touch the melancholic switch in me.

My mother was seated beside me.

"Raghav, how are you feeling now?"

"I'm all right, mom. How did I come here?"

"You had fainted at the airport. Somebody called us, and we had to come to the airport to get you. You never listen to me, you always work too much, and you don't eat properly."

I remained silent. The foremost thought in my mind was that I had to chase Megha again. I felt that my chances of convincing her were highest if I could talk to her as soon as possible. I knew that it would be much harder if I allowed this to drift.

Sachin came to see me later that afternoon. "What happened?" he asked.

"Don't know. I fainted."

"What were you doing at the airport?"

"I had gone to find Megha. She left yesterday. She wrote a letter saying that she wanted to hold the relationship for some time."

"What? Why?"

"She supposedly wants us to concentrate on other responsibilities that we have. And also, her dad is sick."

"Oh. What does she mean by hold? How long?"

"She wants five years."

"What? Five years? Is she mad?"

I was trying hard to stop the tears within me from rolling over the walls of my eyes. I just shrugged.

"I have to go to Pune. I need to find her."

"You've just come home. Wait for a couple of days."

"I need to go as soon as possible."

"Your mom won't allow you to leave home today for sure. Let's see how you're feeling tomorrow."

"Yeah, I know," I said.

"Don't worry, I'll come along. We'll find her. Cool down."

He left after assuring me that things would be all right. I knew that my parents wouldn't permit me to go anywhere immediately. I had to wait.

I didn't have the stomach to digest anything that day, but my mother forced me to eat. My mind was so overloaded with thoughts, and I felt like I would faint again.

Without even wanting to, I fell asleep. And I dreamt of a lot of things that night, a lot of things that I couldn't remember later. But I'm sure they must have been terrible dreams. I wonder if our past and present influence our dreams and whether dreams are the indicators of our future. Or do we have the wherewithal to find new dreams and a new future? I was to find out in the years to come.

Chapter 25

I saw Megha in almost every girl I set my eyes on, that day at the airport. I almost hoped that she would be waiting there, longing for me to come and get her, like it often happens in the climax of more than a few Bollywood movies. But this was no movie. The fairytale script that my heart had written, the beginning of which had seemed to play out perfectly in my life, was somewhat beginning to wither away.

Sachin and I boarded the flight to Pune. He had managed to convince my parents to allow me to go. Somehow, your parents always trust your friends more than you.

The journey through the clouds, sometimes smooth, sometimes stuttering, felt like an endless flight to nowhere. I did not know where to look for her. I did not have her address, her cell phone was switched off and we knew no one else in Pune. Scoring thirty-seven runs of the final over to win a cricket match seemed to be a much better bet than finding her.

Those thoughts circled my loaded mind, as we landed.

"How do you plan to trace her?" Sachin asked, as we were in the taxi travelling from the airport to Pune city.

"I don't know really."

"Hmm... let's see. Do you at least know which part of the city she lives in?"

"No."

He shook his head. "How else can we track her down?" He thought for a few minutes.

"Do you know which college she went to?"

"Yes. We could go there. We may be able to get her address."

Of course it was easier said than done. We did arrive at her college, but we did not know anyone there either. Whom could we ask? We tried to get in touch with someone at the front office, but who would look up records of alumni and pass it on to some stranger? We didn't have a chance.

"I have a friend who studied here; he graduated last year. Let me ask him, he may be able to do something," Sachin said.

He called his friend. I looked around the college campus as he spoke with him. I imagined Megha walking around the campus during her college days.

"He will request one of his juniors to meet us. Let's wait here."

After close to half an hour, a tall boy came towards us. He was very thin, wore an untucked t-shirt and looked like he had just woken up.

"Hi. Sachin?" he asked.

"Yes."

"I'm Arjun. Rohit asked me to meet you. You need some help?"

"Yes, we want to find the address of a former student. Can you please help us?"

"Sure, I can try. Give me the details."

We wrote down Megha's name and year of graduation on a piece of paper and handed it over to him.

"You guys wait here, I'll be back soon. You can sit inside the office if you like."

The college looked very calm, perhaps almost too calm to be the place that housed vibrant young minds. There was a scream or two that could be heard somewhere in the distance, maybe on a playground, or in one of those long corridors that characterize most schools and colleges – those corridors in which a great many memories of our student lives are hung, somewhat like jewels that stud the diaries of the most memorable phase of our lives.

But those rare disturbances died away, much like the odd excitement that withers away in a life destined for melancholy.

We waited there for nearly an hour before Arjun came back. "Sorry to have made you wait so long; here's the address."

He handed us a slip with Megha's address written on it.

"Thanks a lot," I said.

"No problem."

We had an opening. We went back to the taxi and were on our way to Parmar Nagar. It took us a good one hour to reach there.

My heart was beating unbelievably fast as we went up the stairs to her house. The storm that had crept into my life could just die away in one moment of rare fortune, or it could gather further impetus and sweep me away.

I rang the doorbell. After a nearly two-minute wait, just as I had my finger on the bell again, an old man opened the door.

"Is Megha there?" I asked.

"Megha? Who's Megha? Sorry, there's no one by that name here," he said.

"Are you sure uncle?"

"Yes."

"But we were given this address," Sachin said.

"We shifted here about a year ago. Maybe you are looking for old tenants. You can ask around, someone else may know where they moved."

We asked many of the neighbouring houses. A couple of them seemed to faintly remember Megha, but nobody knew where her family had gone.

I was dejected. I didn't know where else we could try. We hung around in Pune for the day, but we knew that we did not have much of a chance of finding her. We went back to the airport. There was no option; there was no way to zero in on her in a decently big city like Pune.

We flew back to Bangalore that night. Back in my room, as I lay on my bed, I reflected on the last two days. Was this the part that I had feared? Was this the curve that I had feared life would throw at me? Was my life going to be a downward spiral from now on?

I was somehow sure that Megha would never come back. And I do not know what came over me. I hit myself on my forehead a hundred times, harder than I had hit anything before. Maybe I wanted to hit my fate. I threw my mobile phone – that expensive smart phone that I had until then managed to protect without a scratch – on to the ground harder than I had thrown anything ever before. It crashed into pieces, much like my life, those scattered pieces on the floor, irretrievable and un-joinable.

I could buy another phone. Perhaps I could buy a hundred more, if necessary. But would I be able to buy another heart?

That was the first deep sorrow in my life. It was heart-breaking. I just let myself free. There was nothing else I could have done. The tears that were inside me came out in an almost unending stream. I wept and wept and wept a thousand tears and more that night. It was as if the walls of my heart had broken and the floodgates had opened uncontrollably.

I don't know if sorrow is memorable. I had lived a great many happy moments with Megha, but maybe melancholy is necessary in life. And sometimes I feel that those moments of intense pain are as memorable as moments of endless joy. Perhaps the depth of life is understood only in the deepest sorrows. Perhaps they do serve a purpose after all.

Chapter 26

I couldn't pick myself up enough to go out of home for one whole week after that. Even though the melancholy in my heart compelled me to believe that I wouldn't see her again, some part of it refused to give up hope. I went to Megha's house to check if her friend knew anything about her. She was at the door, about to leave, when I reached there.

"Hi, I'm Raghav, Megha's friend. Do you know where Megha is?"

"Hi, no, in fact I have been trying to find out."

"Oh."

"I've tried to call her many times. I don't really know why she left so abruptly. She didn't tell me anything," she said. "Yeah," I said.

"Hmm... it's strange."

"Do you know Megha's address in Pune?" I asked.

"No, I don't have her address," she shook her head. "Did she talk to you before leaving?"

"Not completely, she just wrote me a letter that she was leaving."

"Oh."

"I hope you are not hiding anything from me."

"No, I know about Megha and you, and I know how you are feeling. If I knew anything at all, I would have told you. If I get to know about her, I'll inform you."

She recorded my number in her phone.

I tried to get some information about Megha from her now former employer, but that didn't work either. I sent her numerous emails, but got no response. Those were the early days of online social networking, and it hadn't yet picked up to the extent that it has today. Even then, I tried to look for her on a few social networking sites, but couldn't locate her anywhere.

I kept my parents in the dark about what had happened. I wondered if I should tell them, but I was so lost in thoughts and didn't want to complicate things. I went to office after almost two weeks, my mind left with no other option but to drag me there. But for at least a month, I just sat at my desk and did nothing. My friends didn't say anything. They knew that I needed time to get over this.

I slowly started to do some work. I pushed myself to do something. It was the only way to take my mind off what had happened. RS3 had a great foundation. There were challenging days ahead. There were exciting days ahead. I started to realize that the only way I could redeem my life was to excel at work. The only way to bring some happiness into life was to take RS3 to dizzy heights. It would be only a consolation, to be sure, but perhaps a consolation prize is all that I could manage from then on.

Love had failed me. I knew that there was still a little bit of hope left. Megha could keep her word and come back after five years. But it was hard to believe that she would. And I didn't want to fail myself. So even without my heart willing, my mind kept me at bay. I worked and worked and worked, to the extent that I could even find twenty-five hours a day if needed.

And with Sachin, Sandeep and Shantanu also working equally hard, we overturned the feeling of stagnation into unbelievable progress. We raced along crushing every obstacle in our way. RS3 grew bigger and bigger; it became better and better.

If pain can ever be a fuel for something big to grow, I believe that it was in my life. Perhaps my first deep sorrow had indeed served some purpose. I don't know if it brought me happiness. Maybe it didn't. Maybe some souls are not destined for happiness. But it brought me satisfaction. Whether satisfaction is enough compensation for – or perhaps more important than – happiness, is a debate that has often raged within me. But the result has always been inconclusive.

Chapter 27

Within the next four years, RS3 was almost ready to go public. We were nearing five-hundred employees. Gradually, we had diversified and were doing a lot more, though somewhat related to what we had started off with.

Everyone wanted to work for RS3. Gone were the days when we had to chase and convince people to work for us. But that's how it is. People want to be with you when you are on a high; they all want a share of the sweet pie.

We had started with decent ambitions, but we hadn't expected this kind of growth. We hadn't dreamt of such heights. We hadn't expected to catapult to fame and glory this quickly. But we did. Perhaps we had done something right.

Of course we did keep our promise – to ourselves – to always do the right thing. Despite all the social focus, we were still a commercial company. But I can say with great pride that we never once – to the best of our knowledge – swayed from the right path. And I have no doubt in my heart and mind that it contributed a great deal to our success.

Like so many other things in life, doing the right thing is a habit. It was not just the way we did business, it was also the way we lived our lives. You may get away with wrong ways for a few days, maybe even for a few years, but your karma will always hunt you down.

But the real reason for us to be so adamant on following our ideals was not just a hope of some reward. We were tired of people who didn't care about being right. We couldn't watch society slowly but surely going in the wrong direction in the name of business and advancement and growth.

We wanted to show people that success can be achieved in the right way. We wanted to show that it's the only way to real success. We wanted to inspire and bring about a change in peoples' hearts. That was our ultimate reward, not money or fame.

In between all the ideals and success and glory, Megha still remained in every part of me. Thoughts of her inspired me to write poetry. What better than failed love to give birth to your poems?

One night, in one of those moments of poetry in me, I came up with these lines and posted it on my personal blog:

It may be years before I talk to you again,
It may be eternity before I see you again,
But in my heart and in my mind
You'll always remain.

Years will rush past us
And life will go on;
But there will forever remain
Fond memories, of days bygone.

Those cherished moments,
And that feeling so great;
Will Always remain,
Will Never abate.

Destiny brought us together
And silence made us part;
And years later, I still feel
The pain in my heart.

Our lives have taken different paths,
But I Hope someday our paths will meet;

And we will relive those days of old,
So beautiful and sweet!

It helped to feel the pain flow out of me through poetry. It made me feel better, even if only for a few minutes or a few hours. But perhaps it will take me millions of poems and billions of pages and many many lifetimes, to fully put my sorrow into words. And even then, maybe all those lines would only express a small fraction of the ache within me.

I still wept at night sometimes. Love may slowly float down into the ocean of your heart and get hidden by the waters above, but it's still in there, somewhere deep inside. In the endless journey of life it rises back to the surface sometimes. And some other times, we reach deep into ourselves and touch it. And we know that it's still in there. It'll always be there. And so will Megha.

Some of you may think that four years is enough time to recover fully from a deadly blow. It depends on what recovery means. If recovery means leading a normal life, then perhaps you are right. But I had been an idealist in life. I had had great expectations from my life and from myself. Dreams of lofty peaks and perfect journeys had always been a part of me. I couldn't quite forget the bullet that had shot down those high flying dreams of the perfect life.

The "twist" feature on RS3 was still very popular, and it was always in my thoughts, because I often wondered whether we can play God – so to say – and twist our lives the way we want it to be. I wondered whether I would ever be able to turn my life. But there was nothing that I could do. We are not always dealt the cards that we want. We are dealt what we are dealt. We just have to play them in the best way that we can.

And to be fair, fate had given me some good cards as well. The success of RS3 had been nothing short of remarkable. It was a journey that had been romantic in its own way. It was no compensation for lost love – I have struggled to find anything in the world and beyond that is – but it kept me going. And so did the tiny bit of hope that Megha would come back.

PART

TWO

Chapter 28

(Back to) May 6, 2011

As the day slowly meandered along like a river, the memories of those days seemed to stand still, somewhat reflected in the waters of the lake. Yet somehow they faded away into the present.

The long years without her had almost seemed like eternity. I felt that I could not stand another moment without her. Thresholds were almost being reached. Lines of control were almost being breached. It was as if my heart was ready to burst.

Perhaps only those who have loved know what it is to wait, to wait endless aching moments. Only their hearts know how each minute is almost like a lifetime. And yet, the heart summons up the resources to wait one last minute, one last day, one final year. Sometimes I wonder if that is how an inmate in a jail feels like when he is tortured. It was like the heart, crushed by love, in an imaginary jail, being tortured. No escape seemed possible.

Suddenly I heard the sound of a car behind me. I turned back just as the car stopped. My heart must have skipped a thousand beats. "Could it really be her?" As she stepped out, our eyes fell upon each other. For me, that look of hers was like an oasis in the middle of a scorching desert. And it was as if the doors of jail had opened. It was as if an escape route had just become faintly visible. Only, I did not think of the possibility that the oasis could be a mere mirage.

The taxi sped away as she walked towards me, and I could barely move due to my excitement. I felt as if all those years of pain and loneliness were a distant dream. I felt that all the countless tearful nights and those piercing years had been compensated for, in one moment of contact with her eyes.

With a plain red salwar hanging loosely over her body, her hair fluttering in the gentle breeze, small earrings gracing her small ears and the characteristic bindi on her forehead, she looked as beautiful as ever.

But as she drew nearer – our eyes still in contact – I couldn't help but notice how she had changed. Gone was the spark that had lit her once bright eyes. Gone was that wide dimple-enhanced smile that had had the ability to melt hearts instantly. Gone was that incredible charm. Yet, she was still the simple, beautiful girl I had met more than five years ago. Nothing had dimmed her beauty. That undefinable attraction was still intact.

"Hi," she said.

"Hi!" I responded, and hugged her. “I almost thought that you won't turn up".

"I had to keep my promise," she forced herself to a small smile. It was a poor cousin of her former rich version. Yet for me, it was like a glimpse of sunlight after years of being in a dark room, for I had not experienced that smile of hers for so long.

"Thank God you did. I don't know what I would've done if you hadn't come."

"Five years! How have you been?" she queried.

"Well, I've been okay, but how good could I have been without you?"

She looked at me and gave a strange, uncertain look.

"How is your life? You did not call me even once, not even one email in five years. Do you think it was necessary to be completely out of touch?" I asked, trying to hide the anger that had built up within me over the years.

"Life is pretty much normal."

She conveniently ignored my second question and started walking. I followed alongside as we traded pleasantries like it was a formal meeting. The breeze had picked up speed and the rustling of the leaves was louder than our voices. Somehow, the comfort level we had once shared was missing. It was probably natural. Five years is indeed a long time. People change, circumstances change, life itself changes.

"Do you want to sit down?" I asked.

She nodded, and we walked to a bench on the edge of the lake and sat down.

"You don't know how much I searched for you after you left that day. I still can't believe you just left without giving me a chance to talk to you, without even taking my opinion. I don't want to sound like I'm asking for an explanation, and I know that you did tell me in that letter, but what is it that really made you leave suddenly?"

"I will tell you Raghav; I know that I owe you an answer."

After a few moments, she continued, "But let's talk about something else for some time. How is your work? I know your company is doing really well. You are successful and quite well known now. I always knew you would get there. At least one of the reasons for our parting has served its purpose. I'm really happy for you."

I shook my head. "I would trade all the success for five years with you. Hell, I would trade it even for one moment in love with you. You know that."

After a pause I said, "Anyway, we are back together now. I have so much to talk to you about. I have so many things to share with you. I'm sure you also have a lot of stuff to tell me".

She nodded.

"You want to go first?"

She looked into my eyes, the depth of them reflecting a scary hesitation.

"Raghav, I do have something to say to you. I think I should tell you right now. It's not something that you'll like, but I hope you'll understand."

I just looked at her. She was looking down now.

Then, with a voice that almost sounded tearful she said, "Sorry, I couldn't actually keep my promise."

"What do you mean?"

"Raghav, I couldn't keep my promise of love."

She managed to fix her eyes on me for a brief period of time. I looked at her with questions written all over my face. She looked down again. She could not have told me what she was about to, by looking into my eyes.

"I am m...married. I'm really sorry Raghav, circumstances left me with no option," she broke the horrific news, as tears rolled down her eyes.

Those words of hers sent electric shock waves across my body. It shook my roots unlike anything that ever had. I didn't know what to say. I was stunned. My world had crashed once again. This time, there seemed to be no path to recovery. I almost froze. It didn't even sink in. It wouldn't sink in even years later.

Hope is supposed to be the saviour of our wretched lives. It helps us along, making the pangs of pain somewhat bearable. But I often wonder if hope is indeed what wrecks us in the end. Why had I – after so many years – still kept the hope of finding her love again? Maybe it had been a very faint one. Maybe it had just about managed to keep the devils of sorrow from completely taking me away. Yet, when that faint light is crushed by the black darkness, the pain is even more intolerable – if there ever can be a thing that is more intolerable than lost love.

She started weeping uncontrollably. I was aghast. It was she who had wronged me. If anyone had to cry, it was me. What was I supposed to say? What was I supposed to do? I looked to the heavens above as a tear or two rolled down my cheeks. It was without a doubt, the worst moment of my life – the saddest, darkest moment of my life. And I hope that it will forever be, for I cannot imagine how I can bear a pain worse than that.

Dark clouds had gathered in the sky once again. The impending rain seemed like an indicator of the unending tears that were swelling up within me. I don't know why I held them back from a full flow. For me, that moment was almost like a foretaste of death.

"Why are you crying now?" I asked, almost too full of sorrow to even show anger. "You think you have the right to take every decision yourself and just inform me later? You owe me lot more than just an explanation for this one."

Without saying anything, she just wrapped her arms around me, perhaps more tightly than she ever had. And I held her with the tears flowing out. I couldn't help it. Even though the sorrow was almost unbearable, I could perhaps even bear it all over again for that one hug – for just one hug from her. It was still warm – that embrace of hers – almost making the bitter pill of failed love swallowable. Of course it wasn't something that I could actually swallow. I don't know how many lifetimes it will take me – if I ever do – to get over that moment of bitter truth.

It had started to rain slightly, as she began to narrate what had happened. I was about to learn of the sequence of events, those circumstances of her life and perhaps those set of people who had contrived to turn my life upside down.

Chapter 29

May, 2006

(Megha's Side of the Story)

The events that transpired in the days after I left you are not too astonishing. On the face of it, nothing too complex happened. It was almost something that I had expected. But perhaps behind all the plain stories, behind all the simple incidents of our life, are complex emotions that are hard to understand.

The trigger for everything that happened came a few days before I left you. My friend and I visited a well-known astrologer. I used to be somewhat superstitious, and what the astrologer told me was very disturbing. Without even knowing anything about my life or about you, he said that if we stayed together everything would start falling apart in our lives. He told me that there would be serious problems in our relationship, that somebody in my family would fall seriously ill and would die, that your career would be ruined, that our lives will be destroyed. But he also said that this bad phase would last only five years. His advice was that we should not be together for the next five years, that we should not even be in touch. The tone in which he said that was very forceful, as if he could really see that this would happen. Even though it made me feel uneasy, I tried hard not to believe him. But it stayed in some corner of my mind.

A few days after that, I had an argument with my dad. He had found someone who he thought was the perfect match for me, and he wanted me to marry him. I had never really argued with him on anything before that day, but lost in love as I was, I could not help but disagree with him. I couldn't gather enough courage to talk to him about you either. History was against me, for my sister had already experienced that phase. She had been in love with someone from a different community, and despite her desperate attempts to convince dad, he hadn't approved of it. He had even vowed to never see her again if she went against his wishes, and she had to finally agree to let go of her love.

Also, his health had begun to cross the border, from a point of slight uneasiness to one of real worry. He had been suffering from asthma for a few years. What's worse, he was a smoker, and in spite of his condition, he hadn't given it up. I'd tried many many times to coax him, but had failed. With great difficulty, he had managed to stop for a few days after he had had a severe attack, but neglected it every time he got better, and it slowly spiralled into something bigger. And as it often happens, once one part of your body weakens, the others follow. He felt worse with every passing day.

Suddenly what the astrologer had said came back to me. I began to think whether there could be truth in his predictions. Something inside me began to feel that we would be drawn into a whirlpool of negativity and disaster in our lives. And so I made that miserable decision to leave you. I just had to. My mind just couldn't think of anything else. In the first few days after I went back, I did think about returning. I realized the depth of my feelings for you. But I had to resist that urge. Somehow I forced myself to go on.

I had no one to fall back on, except maybe someone deep inside myself. My mother was weak-hearted herself. Shalini – my sister – had plenty of problems in her married life, and she was hardly someone who would lend me anything, let alone a helping hand or a shoulder to cry on.

Maybe I had left the only person whom I could have relied on. I know that I could have come back to you and you would have made it so much easier for me, but it wouldn't have been fair. I had seen the potential that you had had. I knew that you would make it really big, provided you focussed on your work. In the few months we had spent together, I had noticed that you were losing that focus. If I had come to you with all my problems, it would have taken a significant toll on you. I didn't want to be the thorn on your path to success, especially after the prediction from that astrologer.

And so, my heart – lost in a sweet dream, swept away by the force of love – woke up to reality. Sometimes I feel that I should never have allowed my heart to fall in love. When one comes from a conservative family in India, converting love into marriage is hard, and sometimes not even worth the effort. Times have changed, but there's still a long way to go before we as a society cross the line that leaves conservatism behind us. Even though I didn't want to get into it, even though I knew that we may not be able to take it beyond a few feel good days into something concrete, I was somehow drawn to you.

And I let myself fall, in the hope that love will find a way. But after that prediction and my dad falling ill, doubts crept into me. I left you because I didn't want us to get deeper and deeper into ourselves and make it harder to part. Sometimes I feel that I should never have promised you that I would come back. In fact, I was never sure if I would ever return, but I loved you and wanted to keep the hope alive. I hoped that our stars would align more favourably after five years. I hoped that my dad would react positively if I waited till I was a little older. Somewhere in my mind, I knew that it was a selfish decision, but I couldn't help it.

Perhaps I didn't know that I wasn't just waiting for the right time. Perhaps I didn't know that I was running away from facing a difficult situation to a place that was more comfortable. I most definitely didn't know that avoiding the initial discomfort of a tough situation eventually brings great sorrow.

It seems very stupid in hindsight. It seems stupid that I decided to leave you just because of a prediction from some astrologer. But the way things had started to shape up after his strange prediction, left me afraid. It's so true that whatever happens in our lives, it's probably fear that gets us in the end, the fear that prevents us from holding on to what we truly love and believe in.

Luckily, I managed to convince my dad that my marriage could wait for some time. And I found a convenient job, one that paid me well. I didn't bother too much about the work that I had to do, or about building a great career and so on. I wasn't in that frame of mind. As I have told you earlier, I was never in a place where dreams could be born and flourish. I have always admired people like you who dream big and of course achieve them. I could never imagine myself dreaming like that. Maybe I wasn't strong enough for that.

So I went through the motions in my work and in my life. I just waited for things to settle down and get better. I longed to come back to you.

Chapter 30

One day, nearly a year after I had left you, I was sitting in my bedroom, thinking about you. Of course, there was not a day when I didn't think of you. There were days when it made me really sad, and it showed on my face. It was one of those days.

My sister came in to the room. Somehow she never got along with her husband – I wonder whom she got along with – and she used to often stay with us. I too had never had a great relationship with her. She had always felt – without any real reason – that my parents loved me more than her.

Anyway, for the last few days we had at least been talking to each other. As she walked in, she saw me in a pensive mood.

"Something wrong?"

"No," I said, not really wanting to tell her anything.

"But you look sad, I've noticed since morning. C'mon tell me, what happened?" she asked again.

And I don't know why, but something in me decided to tell her. I had to tell someone. I could no longer hold all those emotions in my heart without letting them out.

"There is something I have to tell you."

"What is that? Tell me."

"Well..." I was still contemplating.

"What?"

"It's about someone I met more than a year ago..."

"Huh? Don't tell me..."

"What?"

"You are in love?"

I nodded.

"Oh! Why didn't you tell me till now?"

I looked at her, silently thinking, "What makes you think that I should have told you?" Maybe she recognized those words in me.

But I continued, and told her everything: how we met, how we fell in love, all those wonderful days when we had experienced so much happiness together, and how we parted.

"Why did you leave him like that?" she asked, after I had finished.

"I thought that it was better for both of us to focus on other aspects of our life. We can always get back together."

"Really?"

"Well, frankly I wasn't sure if we could ever take it further."

"So it's your decision. Why are you sad then?"

"Well, I'm missing him."

"Maybe you can go back to him now."

"I can, but it has the potential to put our lives in disarray. And you know how dad is, he wouldn't like it. With him in this state... I don't know..."

"So you're not actually going back."

"I'm confused, but I'd like to think I will."

"Yes, but you shouldn't take this too far. How do you know that he'll wait for you?"

"I don't know, but I hope he does."

"Not everyone finds love Megha. You are so lucky, but you are trying to kill it yourself. You don't realize what you are losing. I still think of... you know who... I still think that I made a mistake..."

"I know. I'll think about it," I said.

"Okay, but don't wait too long."

I was a little surprised at her warmth. As far as I can remember, she had mostly been cold towards me. And being the egoistic person that I am, I had always returned the coldness. But we were sisters, and there were some days when something good took over us and we felt for each other.

But I was suddenly worried that she may share what I had told her with my parents. I couldn't trust her.

"Please don't talk about this with mom and dad."

"I won't. But if you don't do anything for long, I'll tell them."

"Shalini, please don't ever do that. I'll tell them when I think the time is right. You please don't talk about it," I begged.

"Okay, I won't," she assured. She even gave me a warm hug.

Siblings are such important people in our life, and I had always wanted to have a sister who could understand me and be my support. I was happy that I had at least spent a few good moments with her. Happiness is happiness, even if it's short-lived.

Chapter 31

I was in the kitchen with my mother one morning, a few days later, when the doorbell rang. We usually didn't have any visitors. I opened the door, curious to know who it could be. A couple of unfamiliar faces stood outside.

"Yes?" I asked.

"Hello, I'm Raman, an old family friend of Mittal. Is he at home?"

"Yeah, please come in. Dad...," I shouted.

As my dad came out of his room, Mr Raman went and hugged him.

"Raman! It's been so long. Good to see you," my dad said, very happy to meet a long lost friend.

"Yes, somehow couldn't keep in touch after I shifted to Delhi. This is my son, Viren."

"Hello uncle," Viren said.

My dad put an arm around him.

"You were a small kid when I last saw you. Time flies."

"Your daughter?" Mr Raman asked, pointing towards me.

"Yes, Megha."

"Namaste uncle."

After all the introductions and pleasantries – somewhat typical, somewhat sugary, somewhat loud, something that is perhaps unique to India – were done, they settled down. I hung around for a while, not quite knowing what to do.

My mother had gone back into the kitchen; I excused myself and went into my room. As I sat in my room doing random things on my computer, I could hear them talking non-stop. There's so much to say when friends meet after a long time.

After more than two hours or so, my dad called out to me. I came out of my room.

"We're going out for some time," he said, holding his breath, already somewhat tired from the long conversation he had had. Even though it wasn't ideal for him to go out in that state, especially with all the dust outside, I knew that he wouldn't listen to me. So I didn't try to stop him.

"It's almost lunch time," I said, indicating that they should have lunch before they leave.

"I know. But Raman is insisting that we should have lunch outside. Do you want to come along?"

"I have some work to complete."

"Okay."

"Please take your inhaler and take care."

He nodded, and the three of them made their way out of the house. It was good to see my dad in a cheerful mood. I went back into my room and resumed my work.

The meeting of two old friends had somewhat rekindled my thoughts of our reunion. I was tempted more than once during those moments to pick up my phone and dial your number. I almost wonder if destiny didn't want me to.

It was almost evening, and those thoughts had not allowed me to get much work done, when I got a call from my dad.

"Hello." It wasn't my dad's voice.

"Hi, who's this?"

"This is Viren here. Is it Megha?"

"Yes."

"Megha, your dad had an attack, we've admitted him to the hospital."

"Oh. I'm coming," I said and cut the call. I got ready and ran out of the house. I realized that I didn't know which hospital. I was about to call my dad's phone, when Viren called again. It took me more than half an hour to reach the hospital.

"Dad, you should be careful," I said, as I sat next to his bed. These kinds of attacks happened quite often, especially when he went out.

"Yeah."

"Thank you Viren for bringing dad here in time. Where's uncle?" I asked.

"He's gone to meet the doctor."

After that, they visited us often. My dad enjoyed Raman uncle's company. He was always there when my dad needed to go to the hospital for a routine check, or when he just wanted to have a long chat. It helped immensely, to have some support.

Occasionally, Viren and I talked, about my work and the business he had just started. He was a gentle and likeable person. He even asked my dad to work with him, in his business. My dad was more than happy, though of course he couldn't work too much. But it was a welcome change for him.

All along, I often thought of you. Some days, when things seemed slightly bright at home, I had thoughts of getting in touch with you. But somehow, I couldn't make up my mind. I heard of your company beginning to really flourish. I didn't want to ruin your momentum.

I often wished for a wand that would – with one short or long swish – instantly make you appear in front of me. Perhaps that wand was always with me. Perhaps it was just a phone call away. Perhaps we don't really need any special wand in life.

Chapter 32

"Megha, what do you think about Viren?" my sister asked me one day.

"What? What about him?"

"Do you like him?"

"What? Are you mad? You know that I love someone else."

"Yeah yeah, I saw Viren and you talking to each other so much yesterday. I've seen you two together quite a few times. Who knows, maybe you've changed your preference."

It didn't take long for the anger in me to show up when she was with me, and I frowned at her. She was like that; she couldn't stand it if things were going along smoothly, especially for me. After that talk with her when I had told her everything about us, I had begun to feel that things were all right between her and me; but that question of hers irritated me no end.

"Since you are not in touch with Raghav and you are enjoying Viren's company so much, I thought you might like him," she said, smiling. I hated that smile.

"Will you shut up. I still love Raghav," I said, raising my voice.

"Come on Megha, I'm just telling you what I think. Don't get angry. If you still like Raghav, why don't you go back to him?"

"You please don't bother. I'll do that when I want to," I shouted.

"Why are you shouting? Cool down. I can talk to mom and dad if you want me to. Maybe I can help you." Her face almost seemed to smile at me, even though she wasn't actually smiling.

"Get lost," I shouted. She walked out of my room. My sister was an eccentric sort of a person. One never knew what she would do; even she didn't know. Sometimes, she even found a strange joy in ruining other peoples' happiness.

I was in my parents' room one evening, a few days after that fight with my sister. It had been more than a year and a half since the day I left you. My sister was also present.

"Megha, I have some good news for you," my dad said.

"Good news? What good news?"

"You know Viren, Raman's son..."

"Yes."

"He likes you. Raman had come home yesterday to ask for your hand. I'm really happy," he said.

It sunk me. "What? But dad..."

"You don't like him?" my mom asked.

"It's not like that, but..."

"I know you also like him," my dad interrupted me. "I've seen you talking to him many times. Shalini also told us about it."

My mind went blank. From head to toe I was seething with anger towards my sister. If she hadn't told them anything, it would have been easier to put forth my views. But she had put me in a really difficult spot. I couldn't say anything instantly.

My dad sensed the confusion in me, perhaps even the rejection of his decisions.

"Even if you feel that you're not sure, I'm sure that this is good for your future. Don't you think that I know what's best for you?" he asked.

"Give me some time to think," I said, and came away.

My sister came to my room after a few minutes.

"So, what are you thinking?" she asked.

"What should I think? You ruined it by telling dad stupid stories. When did I tell you that I like Viren?"

"Didn't you hear what dad said? He said it's best for you."

"How...," I was about to question how my dad knew what's best, when I stopped myself.

"And it's not like you don't like him at all. He's a good man and you shouldn't be losing him thinking of some old love that you lost yourself," she said in an irritating voice.

"Did you tell dad about Raghav?" I was afraid that she had spilt the beans.

"How does it matter now? Did dad ask you about it?"

"No. Maybe he doesn't want to give me a chance to convince him. But did you tell him?" I shouted.

I waited for her to answer. My blood boiled. With no answer forthcoming, I became so furious that without even knowing it I got up from my bed and pushed her. She didn't go away, and I stared at her for more than a few seconds.

"Megha, why are you getting angry?"

I continued to stare at her, and she walked out of the room.

"What has she done?" I thought. I sometimes wonder if she did that because of her failed love story. Perhaps she didn't want mine to succeed as well. It was a terrible thought, but she was capable of that.

Even though you and I had been apart for so long, I had always hoped that we would be back together someday. I knew you loved me, and I was sure of my feelings for you. But that night, for the first time, I was worried.

Chapter 33

I was on the terrace one day, just reflecting on the direction my life was taking. I heard a voice call out to me.

"Hi Megha, how are you?"

I turned around and saw Viren standing behind me.

"Hi, I'm okay."

We had a slow conversation, interspersed with generous doses of calm. Then, he asked me what I feared he would.

"Megha, did your parents talk to you?"

"About what?" I said, defensively.

"Oh, I thought they had," he mumbled.

I realized that I couldn't push away the matter.

"Yes, they did," I said, looking down.

"Oh, good. Actually, I wanted to talk to you before approaching your parents, but Shalini gave me enough hints that you also..."

"What? That devil..." I thought. All the doubts that I had had about my sister's role in it were confirmed.

Viren was staring at me. I had often noticed him looking at me, far more than anyone normally would, but I hadn't thought much about it. I decided that I should tell him the truth immediately.

"So...?" he asked.

"Viren..." I was about to tell him, when my mother cried out.

We both ran down stairs. My dad had collapsed. We rushed him to the hospital. This wasn't the usual asthma attack. Over the next few days they conducted various tests on him. He was all right, but was really weak.

"We've carried out all important tests," the doctor said, as Viren and I sat in his chamber. "Generally, all his parameters are not too good. He really has to give up smoking. This is a huge red signal and a sign that other parts of his body are giving way. If he doesn't act now, it'll be too late."

I stepped into my dad's room that evening, as he lay on his bed. He had insisted on going back home early.

"Dad, how are you feeling now?" I put my hand on him. He sat up, slowly adjusting his weakened body against the pillows.

"I'm fine," he said with a wavering, unclear voice.

"No, you are not. You have to stop smoking."

The wrecks of many cigars he had smoked lay in the ash tray that sat on a table nearby, next to a half-used pack. What power those small sticks can hold over a man, almost like a master controlling his slave! I hated the sight of them.

"Yeah, I'm trying."

"That's not good enough anymore. You just HAVE to stop. NOW."

He just stared into the distance, across the room.

"I'll..." He started coughing uncontrollably. I helped him with a glass of water. He signalled to me that he wanted to lie down.

I looked at him as he closed his eyes. He looked extremely weak. My hands were tied now. I couldn't possibly speak to him about us. It was going to be very hard to refuse if he asked me about Viren again. Even though my dad was a soft person, he was strict. He wouldn't have taken it lightly if I had told him our story.

I had to find a way out of it. I thought hard; there had to be some way. I could have talked to Viren, but I didn't know if it would help. And I couldn't do it immediately, especially with dad's health still very much on the edge. And so, with my dad's collapse that day, my world collapsed.

Why do we go down a path when we know that it may not have a future? Why do we fall in love when we know that we will eventually have to part? Why do we continue to love, even when there is no hope left?

Chapter 34

My dad came to my room the next day. I was tense. I knew that the question was coming.

"Have you thought about it?"

"About what?"

"About Viren, who else? I know that there is nothing to think about, but I still wanted to ask you."

And I don't know how a force of courage built up inside me. I don't know what happened to me. I decided to tell him about you.

"Dad, there's a reason why I don't want to marry Viren."

"What is that?" He was looking at me keenly.

"I love someone else."

"What??" His reaction was as if it was impossible for me to fall in love with anyone.

"I wanted to tell you earlier, but..."

"Who is it? What's his name?"

"Raghav. I met him in Bangalore."

Without even letting me tell him my story, he just walked out.

"Dad..." I called out, but he didn't turn back.

A few hours later, my dad had calmed down, and we were seated outside a temple. He wanted to talk to me.

"There's something I haven't told you," he started. "It's something that may shake you up. It's a secret that your mother and I have held on to for so long."

I didn't say anything. I didn't know that my life was about to take a totally unexpected turn.

"You are not our biological daughter."

I turned towards him, my body almost paralysed with the shock from those words.

"Uhhh?"

"We found you..."

"What?? Dad, are you joking?"

"No," he said, with a shake of his head.

"Where did you find me? Who are my real parents?" My voice was shaking.

He proceeded to tell me the details of the secret of my life that had been buried for so long. It was a secret that I would never have wanted to know. The details of how they found me and how it changed my fate don't matter here; I'll tell you some other time. But it crushed me, that revelation of his. It really did. I couldn't withhold the tears that flowed endlessly from my heart that couldn't quite accept what it had heard. But what crushed me further were his words after that.

"We have done so much for you, we have given you a good life, and here you are now, a grown up girl not even respecting our decisions. Do you even realize where you would have been if we hadn't accepted you as one of our own?"

It was almost as if he was asking me to abide by his decisions to repay him for all that he had done for me. I had had great respect for my dad, but somewhere in that moment, at least a small part of that respect died. I still loved him, as much as love can exist without respect, but I didn't feel good at all.

That day was such a disaster. It just rips you apart, the knowledge that you have never seen your actual parents, the knowledge that the people whom you thought were your parents are actually strangers in a way, strangers who helped you and whom you have to be indebted to for life. That stunning revelation ruined my peace forever.

Later that night, I went to my dad's room. I wanted to do something to feel better. I went and just hugged him unable to control the emotion.

"Dad... I want to tell you that I will always do whatever you want me to do."

"I know you. I knew that you will never disrespect me." He was so relieved.

It's strange that many parents believe that their children don't respect them if they don't accede to their wishes. It was ironical, because I had acceded to his wishes after losing some part of the great respect that I had had for him.

And I never brought up the topic of me not being their real daughter after that. I didn't even want to be reminded about it. I just wanted some peace.

Viren called me the next day.

"Thank you for saying yes! I'm so happy!"

"Umm..."

"It means a lot to me Megha. I'll always keep you happy."

I didn't know what to say. I hung up somewhat abruptly after a few minutes of mostly one-way talk. It was definitely beginning to get out of hand. I was feeling like the door was being bolted. I wondered whom I could talk with. The only option I thought I had was to call you, and I almost did. But I knew that it would only complicate matters. Also, it had been so long. Maybe you had moved on. Maybe you had found someone else. Maybe you had forgotten me.

And so the wedding date was set. Even then, I had some hope that a miracle would turn it all around, maybe a moment of divine intervention, maybe an inspired moment when I just made up my mind to run away.

Chapter 35

There was a festive look in Viren's house on the eve of our wedding. Although most weddings are held in big marriage halls, hotels, or at times at the brides' place, our ceremony was scheduled to be held there, since they had a big house.

We landed there at seven in the morning. I couldn't believe that I was dressed up as a bride. The next day was supposed to be the most memorable day of my life – the day of my wedding, the day when I was supposed to look the most beautiful I had ever looked. Maybe I did look beautiful – Viren kept looking at me – but there was no beauty inside me.

There were plenty of rituals, some inexplicable things that I had to do, some alone, some with Viren and some with my parents... after some time I stopped recollecting with whom and also stopped counting.

And there was dance, music and celebration. There were smiles, good wishes and loads of excitement. And of course, amongst all that, was the turmoil in my heart. All along, I saw the happiness on my parents' faces and felt some satisfaction. It somehow kept the fire burning deep inside my heart at bay.

"Are you happy, Megha?" my mother asked me, as I slept with my head on her lap, later that night. Why do parents do what they want, make all the decisions for us, and then ask us whether we are happy? Are they really concerned, or is it just a strange feeling of guilt inside them?

"Doesn't matter."

"What do you mean by doesn't matter?"

"Let's say that I'm not happy, what will you do?"

"Megha, why are you not happy?"

"Now I don't want you to convince me that I am happy or that I should be happy. Let it just be," I said, getting up.

"God! Don't know what else she wants."

"Nothing. Good night."

Back in my room, I stood near the window. It was nearing midnight. There was no moon that night, as if to signify the darkness in my life. Everything was calm outside.

I was about to set foot on a path from which no return seemed possible. I thought that it wasn't really my choice. I thought about what you used to say about the choices we make, and about life being our responsibility. I realized that I was probably scared to make a choice. I was scared to take responsibility for the events in my own life. And ironically, that was also a choice that I had made.

I stared outside, into the distance far away. I saw images of you in that direction. Perhaps you were also looking at me. I felt as if I was sharing that moment of sorrow with you. I couldn't control myself; I had to cry.

It was undoubtedly the darkest day of my life. And the future – if there was any – was even darker.

There were more ceremonies and rituals on the day of the wedding. I had been to other weddings and had wondered how people sat through all of them. And there I was, trying my best to maintain my calm through the whole thing. It was almost unbearable for me, especially because it wasn't a marriage of hearts.

Again, there were all the same visitors, plenty of them. Everyone wanted to meet us and bless us. It irritated me a little bit as I thought about it. "Bless" is a strange word. Do people bless us so that we can really get what we truly want? Does God bless us so that we can realize our dreams and live the life we want, or does He "bless" us so that we can bear the life that He has written for us?

I looked at Viren on and off. He looked so happy. I wondered if he knew that I didn't want to marry him. Perhaps he would have stepped back if he knew about it. But I could see that he loved me, and love makes us do things we wouldn't normally do. We want to be with people whom we love even if they don't love us. Deep in our hearts, we know that we can never have them, but we still love them and want them.

I constantly closed my eyes during the final moments of the wedding, unable to believe that it was actually my wedding with someone other than you. I still hoped that at the last moment – at the very last moment – something would happen and save me. But sadly, not every story has a favourable twist.

In between, I saw my dad who still looked unwell – even though he was happy – and all hopes of a dramatic revival of my fortunes died.

Many of the guests had brought us presents. Some of them gave us bouquets of beautiful red roses. I wondered if they signified colour and softness, or thorns in my life. I wondered if one of those boxes, inside those pretty papers, could contain one wish for me – one wish that would grant me the permission to flee from all this. Of course I didn't need permission from anyone other than myself. We don't ever need permission from anyone else in life. It's strange that we think otherwise.

And so, Viren and I were married – not the right word perhaps, considering that it was just a wedding. But at least in the eyes of the world we were married.

In the days following our wedding, Viren realized that I didn't love him. In the same way that you can't hide true love, you can't fake it where there is none. And he let me be; we just stayed together. I felt sad that I had ruined his life too, but then, there was nothing I could have done.

I knew that he hoped I would change someday. It showed in his eyes and in his actions. Gradually, we became friends, but there was always that bit of uneasiness between us. Perhaps somewhere, there still is. But we never talked about it.

I must say that he was incredibly patient with me, and I was thankful for that. A life with someone you don't love is bad enough; I couldn't have survived if that someone had turned out to be a jerk.

Every now and then, I had thoughts of telling him about us; I had thoughts of breaking away from him. But it was hard to do that to him. Also, those days with you seemed so long ago that I doubted if there was any use of hoping for a life with you.

My career was going along nicely. I was never too good at it in the beginning, but I learnt to do whatever I had to, sufficiently well. And it was some consolation – a very very small consolation.

The days passed by, and I let my life drift away, allowing the wind to carry me to wherever it deemed fit, to wherever my destiny lay.

PART

THREE

Chapter 36

(Back to) May 6, 2011

The consistent drizzle was still on. It hadn't stopped raining in my life. Megha had been looking down throughout her narration, and she turned to look at me now. I knew that she was trying to gauge my reaction. I hadn't openly reacted to her story. I didn't know how to react. Even though I felt – and knew – that her story was genuine, I still thought that there should have been a way out of it. I couldn't imagine that leaving me then was the only option that she had had.

But whatever the reasons, whatever the circumstances, we couldn't go back. Whatever happens in life, however sad you are, there's one thing that's certain: you can't have a better past. However much you want to, you can't. It's one of the truest truths in life, but also the one that's the most difficult to accept.

I could have debated about why she had left me, about why she had chosen the path that she did, but I was too shaken to even think about it. I almost felt like killing her. I felt like tearing my hair out. I felt like smashing everything in my way.

"What should we do now? How should we say farewell? With a kiss? A hug? Tears?" I said, making the sarcastic tone quite apparent, as I got up.

I could have sympathized with her, perhaps I should have. But her story was far too bitter for me, and I couldn't find any sweetness inside.

"Raghav, can't we part with good memories? Can't we part with good wishes?" she asked.

"Megha, I'll always wish you well."

She may have wronged me in a way; I may have hated her for that; but I still loved her. I still loved her from the deepest part of my heart and soul. If I tried to pull out those roots that had grown into my heart, they would only hurt me more; they could never ever be pulled out completely. And even if they were detached by some miracle, the scars that they would leave would be indelible.

"Thanks Raghav, I know that. But I also want you to move on in life. I want you to have a good and happy life. We had a great time together then and we'll always have wonderful memories of those days, but your future lies in not dwelling too much on the past."

And we remained silent for the next few minutes, the words we could not speak and the sorrows we could do nothing about almost floating around our ears and hearts.

"Are you going back to Pune today?"

She was a little surprised by the tone of that question. She nodded.

"I'll take you to the airport," I said, as I started walking towards the car. Her eyes had begun to emit fresh tears. The tone of my voice and my behaviour was hurting her. I didn't want to hurt her, but I was reeling from the wound which she, in combination with fate and destiny, had inflicted on me.

The light of the evening was beginning to fade, and with those last rays of light, my last hopes of a happy life too evaporated into the air. The rain drops still fell softly onto the grass as Megha and I walked towards the car together, perhaps for the last time.

Chapter 37

We were on our way to the airport as night descended upon us. I stole glances at Megha, much like I had done when I had been with her on our first date, now many years ago. She still looked unbelievably beautiful. My heart couldn't get over the fact that it would have to beat without her. And I filled my heart and mind with images of her – images that would last a lifetime.

Just then, I remembered something. I stopped the car on the side of the road.

"What happened?" she asked.

I turned on the light inside the car, reached behind and pulled out the flowers that I had kept on the back seat. I hadn't been sure that she would turn up that day, so I had only brought along some flowers.

"Happy Birthday!" I said, as I held them near her.

"You remembered! Thank you," she said, as she accepted the flowers.

"Of course, how could I forget," I said, as our eyes met.

And somewhere in that moment of small celebration and non-existent reunion, those lonely and almost endless intervening years sandwiched between the past and the present were dissolved, my heart travelling back to that day of celebration and parting, years ago.

We regained our senses as those years between us came back to separate us. We both didn't quite know what to say after that. I started the engine and we were on our way again.

"Raghav, can I ask you something?" Megha queried after a few minutes of silence.

"Yeah?"

"If I say that I am in trouble, will you help me?"

It was a strange question. I just looked at her not knowing what to say. She looked back at me as if silently repeating the question.

"What is it, tell me?"

"I have a serious problem. I'm in a big mess."

"Huh? What happened?" I asked, seriously concerned. I almost halted the car again, but drove on slowly.

"If you promise to help me, I will tell you."

I felt that she would not have told me anything if I hadn't wished her. It had suddenly made us somewhat more comfortable with each other. Somewhere my heart wondered if she had come back to meet me with the intention to seek help. I wondered if she would never have come if she didn't need something from me.

"Please believe me when I say that I didn't come here to ask for your help. I came here to meet you, to keep my promise, whatever was left of it", she said, as if she had read my mind.

Even though I had a hint of doubt, I still chose to believe her.

"I believe you."

"I don't really know how you will help me. In fact, I'm really embarrassed to ask for your help after all that I have done, but you are someone I can depend on."

"Yes Megha, please tell me what happened."

"I'm facing a criminal case."

"Criminal case? What are you saying?" I was shocked.

I stopped the car. We were still outside the city.

"Tell me what happened," I said.

"Actually, it's worse. It's a murder case."

"What? Murder case? You killed someone?"

The level of shock within me rose up several notches higher. I looked at her. It was hard to believe that such a cute girl had been the cause of someone's death.

"It was a sort of accident. I didn't mean to kill, but there is sufficient circumstantial evidence against me, and now I'm almost doomed.

I've tried everything, but there seems to be no way out of this. You are the only one I can ask for help now," she said, her voice showing that she was frightened.

"How did it happen?" I asked.

"I will tell you, but how do you think you can help me?"

"You have to first tell me what happened. Of course I'm not a lawyer, but maybe I can do something."

"I'm actually not allowed to leave Pune because of the case. I've only come here for a day, with permission. If you have to help me, you will have to come to Pune. Can you?"

Thoughts of refusing her request came to me, but I knew of no way of saying no to the woman I loved. And the chance to meet her again, to be with her again, even if temporarily, was too inviting for me.

I found it strange that she asked me for help. I found it strange that she wanted me to still be involved in her life. Maybe she still loved me. Maybe.

"Okay, I'll come. You know that I'm always going to be there for you."

"Thank you Raghav. I'll tell you everything when you are there."

My mind kept telling me not to have anything to do with her, and I knew that it was good advice. But fresh drops of hope had started appearing somewhere deep in the ocean of my heart. My mind knew that there was no future in this. But the heart that loves does not think about logic or rationale; it always hopes, it always loves.

I saw her off at the airport, with the promise to go to Pune in two days. She gave me her phone number. I finally had her number again, more than five years after I had first had it. We were finally going to be in touch again, exactly five years after we had lost it.

It had been such a bizarre day. I had experienced more emotions that day, than I had ever experienced in my whole life. There had been more twists and turns than I could have fathomed. I could not quite comprehend what life was trying to tell me. They say life sends you messages in various ways, through people, through coincidences and perhaps through every little and seemingly insignificant thing.

I thought about what life was trying to convey. I hadn't had too much hope that Megha would actually turn up that day; I had virtually given up. But she did come. I had felt as if my soul had come back to life again. Life didn't like that, and it threw one of those punches at me. And in a moment, all my hopes had disappeared again. Just as I had accepted my fate, a silver line had appeared somewhere.

Maybe life was trying to tell me that I shouldn't give up. Every time I had tried to do that and closed the door, a ray of hope had come in through a window somewhere. And even without my conscious mind knowing it, I decided that I would try to win Megha's heart again.

I should have been more concerned about helping her get out of the situation that she was in. It wasn't that I didn't care about it; I did. But I wanted more than just a solution to her problem. I wanted a solution to my problem. I wanted her back. And perhaps the solution to my problem lay in solving hers.

I knew that it was not the best thing to do. I knew that she was married. It shouldn't even have figured in my possibility map. It wasn't even in line with the "right" way. But as I have said earlier, love knows no logic. It has its own reasons. It had taken over me. And so, a drowning person had been thrown a lifeline.

Chapter 38

With the doors of love reopened in my mind, and the rays of hope making their way through the windows of my heart, I landed in Pune two days later. I wonder if the doors and windows of our hearts and minds have anything to do with the doors and windows of life. I wonder if there is a place – even imaginary, somewhere far away – where they converge.

On my way from the airport to the city, I remembered that day, five years ago, when I had frantically searched for her. I checked into a hotel and called her.

"Hello."

"Hi Megha, I just arrived."

"Great. I will see you in a couple of hours in the hotel." I had already given her the details.

"Okay."

In the room, I lay on the bed and closed my eyes. I thought of the strange turn my life had taken. And lost in those thoughts, I fell asleep. The ringing sound of my phone woke me up some time later. Megha was calling.

"Hello."

"Hi, I'm waiting in the lounge."

"Okay, I'm coming."

I made my way out the room, down the staircase, towards the lounge. As I walked towards Megha seated there, I spotted someone else seated next to her. Both of them got up as I drew nearer.

"Hi, this is my husband, Viren."

"Hi Raghav, nice to meet you."

"Hi."

It felt very strange to meet her husband. It's hard to describe that moment in words, but it was a difficult moment for me. It was hard to stand in front of the person who had been instrumental in crushing my love. It was impossible not to feel a certain hatred towards him.

He was of medium build, somewhat fair and taller than me. He had longish hair. And – I feel somewhat hesitant to accept this – he seemed to be a good man. How can the husband of the woman you love – unless it's you yourself – be a good man?

We sat down and spoke a few words. Megha did most of the talking, but I could see that she was also feeling very awkward. Viren left after a while.

"Have you told him about us?" I asked Megha after he was gone.

"No, I told him that you were my classmate."

"Why didn't you tell him the truth?"

"Well, I'm not sure. I didn't know what to tell him; I didn't know how to tell him."

"Okay. So tell me, what happened?" I asked, my mind now terribly anxious to know how she had ended up being accused in a murder case.

She was about to speak when I interrupted her. "Do you want to talk about it here or shall we go to my room?"

She looked at me hesitantly.

After a pause she said, "Okay, let's go to your room". We went up to my room in the eighth floor. We stood in the balcony. There were not too many taller buildings in that direction, and we could see far away into the city and beyond.

"I was in my sister's house one day," she began. "It was about four months ago. As you already know, my sister and I don't get along too well. Also, I somehow feel that she was responsible for my wedding with Viren. I've hated her even more since then. We've also had other issues with each other, though I've never understood exactly what it was that bothered her.

"She had invited me home that day. She wanted to sort things out. Though I didn't really want to talk to her, I went, because I didn't want her to come home and complicate things. It was all right in the first few minutes. She started talking about general stuff, about her paintings and so on. I didn't care too much, and I tried hard to tolerate her.

"But as she went on talking, I got the feeling that she was making an effort to be friendly. She wasn't making sarcastic comments or talking rough like she usually did. It was as if she had been transformed into someone else. It made the conversation warm – more so because of the hot cup of coffee – and peaceful.

"After a while, I asked her about her husband. She had not been staying with him for a few weeks. As I have already told you, they had never really seemed compatible with each other. Though she did not like me asking about him, she didn't show any anger. She politely told me that she didn't want to talk about it.

"I had always felt that she was the one who had caused all the problems in her marriage. Until that day, I had resisted discussing that with her. But looking at the calmer side of her that day, I made the mistake of letting her know what I felt. I told her that she needed to be more accommodating. It was stupid of me. Why was I trying to put sense into her senseless mind?

"Slowly, but surely, things heated up. She lost her cool. She started raising her voice. I somehow controlled my anger. I just wanted to get up and leave. Then, just like I had started a topic that she didn't like, she brought up something that was very uncomfortable for me.

"She began to question my love for you and how she felt that I had not hesitated to cheat you. I was shocked, especially because of the feeling that she had been partly responsible for ruining our chances. Lots of times before that day, I had felt like holding her neck and strangling her.

"Anyway, she even started using a few abusive words. I was finding it hard to control my anger now. I knew that it was best for me to leave immediately; I didn't want this to get out of hand. I stood up and turned around to go, but she caught hold of my dress and stopped me.

She was on her feet now. I turned back and pushed her. She still stood her ground. The temper and irritation inside me just burst out, and in one moment of rage, I pushed her with greater force.

"She fell backwards and her head first hit hard against a table covered with glass and then against the floor with a thud. I suddenly realized what I had done. I knelt down and shook her, I cried out to her; but she didn't respond. She was dead. I was flabbergasted at what had happened. My sister was dead. I had killed my own sister! I didn't know how to react to the situation.

"I left her body there and went away. Of course, I was eventually caught. There was enough evidence in the house, like my fingerprints in various places and on her body. To add to that, many people knew that my sister and I didn't get along well, and my mother was aware of my visit to her place that day.

"I was petrified. As if my life didn't have enough problems. I didn't know how to get out of the hole that I had dug for myself."

She still looked horrified, as she completed the story. It was as if she was still living that experience.

"Sometimes I feel pretty hollow that I killed my own sister. But then other times I don't care. She had always hated me and had even complicated my life so much. But moments after I have a 'don't care' kind of feeling, I begin to hate myself. Because how can I kill someone and not care?

"Anyway, the case has been on in court, though they have let me off temporarily on bail. Though there is enough evidence, my lawyer has been trying to prove that there is some doubt. But I've started feeling that I will be convicted."

I stood there almost paralyzed. She had killed her sister? She had actually killed her sister? Megha wasn't a person whose temper flared easily. So I was even more surprised and stunned at what she had done. Yes, her sister had not been too kind to her. Yes, it was a sort of accident. But still, to kill anyone – let alone your own sister – is pretty sad. I wondered what to say.

"Megha, I can't believe that you killed your own sister."

She nodded. "Sometimes, even I can't believe it. But it just happened."

The city looked beautiful from there. Every house seemed to be calm. From afar, everything and every place looks peaceful. Only when we look closely can we see the cracks. Only when we go into a house and dissect it, can we feel the uneasiness that exists inside. And I thought about another possible storm that was about to erupt in my life.

"What should we do now Megha? How can I help you?"

"I don't know; I'm lost. Sometimes I feel that maybe I deserve this."

I didn't know how to respond to that. I knew that she was at fault. Whatever the circumstances, however much you are angry, there is no excuse for taking someone's life, even if by accident or in the heat of a moment.

I had somewhat hated her when had she left me. I had really hated her when she had told me about her marriage. But I had still believed that she was a good person. I had thought that she was still innocent. But after what she told me that day, I looked into her eyes, and it seemed to me that her innocence was gone. Perhaps it hadn't gone anywhere. Perhaps it was still inside her. Perhaps it was just the shock of that story that made me feel that way.

I even thought about letting her know of my feelings. Ethically speaking, I should not have even thought of helping her. But one thing stopped me. It didn't let me tell her the truth. It even made me take paths that I would otherwise never have taken. It was that old feeling. That grand old thing called love. I know that love is blind, but when I think of those days, I wonder if love is sometimes deaf as well. It must have been, because it didn't hear the unending cries of someone deep within me to stop. I had to help her. My love for her had to win.

"No Megha, as you said, it was an accident. It wasn't as if you did it intentionally," I tried to comfort her.

"Let's see how you can get out of this," I added.

"Thanks, Raghav. And I'm sorry to have dragged you into this, especially after all that I've done to you," she said apologetically.

"Let me think about how I can help you here. I'm sure we'll find some way to prove your innocence."

"Thanks," she said again, and held my hands. I felt weird; it was confusing. Did she actually still love me? It drove me crazy, in a different sort of way. In old times, that touch of hers would have generated a stream of wonderful sparks. But now, I was feeling more and more uneasy. I had gone there with thoughts of bringing her back into my life, yet that touch somehow didn't generate positive vibes in me.

Chapter 39

I didn't sleep well that night. Perhaps I'd never had a good night's sleep ever since Megha had left me. But the confusion in my mind that night added to the sleeplessness. It was only in the early hours of the morning that I managed to doze off, and I didn't wake up till noon.

I decided to use the whole of next day to go around the city. I wanted to be alone for a while. I wanted to gather my thoughts. Exploring a city by foot is one of the most amazing experiences. It's so true that as you discover the world outside, you also discover the world within. And that day, as I explored the city, I also explored my innermost thoughts.

I walked along a busy main road, as the traffic breezed past me in either direction. It was like those vivid memories of the past that swayed to and fro in my head. I didn't quite know which way to go, and I just trudged along.

I covered quite some distance somewhat unconsciously, with the noise of the city almost drowned in the inner noise of my mind. I came to what looked like a newly built restaurant that opened into the main road, the scents and colours of the rush outside somehow merging seamlessly into the interiors. I walked inside and took a seat overlooking the road. It was almost half past one and I hadn't even had breakfast.

The menu had a lot of options, and I just ordered something random. As I was waiting for my lunch to arrive, I looked around the restaurant and couldn't help but observe the different people and the varied expressions on their faces.

There was a large group that had occupied what seemed like at least five joined tables in the centre. They seemed to be part of an extended family. The children were looking indifferent, as the adults enjoyed the food. On another table, a little distance from them, sat a couple. One could almost sense that they were newly married; they were constantly looking at each other and smiling.

In the corner, on the far side sat three middle-aged men, engrossed in what was perhaps a business meeting. They were constantly talking and seemed to be having fervent discussions.

Everyone was lost in their own thoughts, in their own world. Observing the behaviour of different people is interesting. It's interesting to watch their ways and mannerisms and to try and comprehend them. I had never grown tired of that.

My food arrived and I gulped it down quickly as I was hungry. But it was tasteless, and I didn't relish it. When we are overwhelmed by melancholy and confusion, and when life itself seems bitter, nothing tastes good.

My thoughts were interrupted by the sound of my phone. It was Megha.

"Hi Raghav, what are you doing? I called you three–four times."

"Hi Megha. I woke up late and I just came out to have lunch. Sorry, I didn't notice that you had called."

Amongst my complicated thoughts, I hadn't heard my phone. I had missed her calls.

"My lawyer wants to meet you; can we meet today?" she asked.

"We can, but I fixed up a meeting with a friend in the evening. Sorry. If it's urgent we can meet today. If not, can we meet tomorrow morning?" I wanted to think before meeting her lawyer.

"That's okay, let's meet tomorrow. Ten?"

"Yeah."

I was hoping all along that no one would recognize me. After all, RS3 was a well-known company now, and people knew me. Just as I was thinking about it, a man came up to me.

"Mr Raghav!" he exclaimed, as he held out his hand. He said it so loudly that everybody around turned to look at us.

Reluctantly, I shook his hand.

"I'm so glad to meet you like this. I've always admired RS3 and the way you have built up everything over the last few years," he said, swallowing some of the words in his excitement. I had never dreamt that someday, someone random would be excited to meet me. But the success of RS3 had indeed made all of us popular.

I smiled.

"Can I sit down here?" he asked.

I was a little irritated, but I couldn't show it. He started talking about himself and went on and on. He also spoke about RS3 and his thoughts, both positive and negative. Some people continued to look at us on and off. Finally, he told me that we wanted to visit RS3's office and talk to me more about some of the ideas he had.

However big you grow, however famous you become, I've always believed that your attitude towards the people you meet, especially strangers, should be pleasant and accommodating. And I've always personally given time, even without prior notice, to anyone – well, almost anyone – who wanted to meet me. You never know when someone will bring in an idea, or some thought or some opportunity that can change you for the better. I was only irritated that day because I was filled with so many thoughts. And I would have even had an interesting chat with that man if it was not for my mental state.

I gave him my card and asked him to call me. He was satisfied and left. I quickly made my way out of the restaurant, and continued my walk. The chances of people recognizing me while walking on the street were much lesser.

I came to a traffic signal that had four intersecting roads. I looked at each of them and took the one that looked the least busy. It occurred to me that I was perhaps at crossroads in my life. Pushing that thought aside, I went on, soaking in the atmosphere of the city.

And I walked on and on, stopping at various points, as the afternoon turned into evening. After a time, I came across a pretty large park. It was calm and scenic, and the evening breeze and atmosphere made it look even more lovely. I went inside and sat down on a bench. It was sparsely populated.

I realized that I hadn't even come close to any conclusion about Megha. How would I help her? Should I even help her? I debated long and hard to understand whether Megha was actually at fault. Did she deserve punishment?

Whenever I thought about this, my thoughts quickly turned towards my feelings. I still loved her, and I knew that she had some feelings for me. How could I see the love of my life in trouble and not help her?

I went back to the hotel room, my mind clouded with a hundred such questions.

Chapter 40

Megha arrived the next morning, along with her lawyer. He was a stout, proud man. He wore a cap – I couldn't quite ascertain if he was bald – and by the way he spoke, I could sense that he had been involved in many a false case. He had an idea about how I could assist them.

"Sir, there is one way you can help," he said, as we sat in the restaurant, which was located on the ground floor of the hotel.

"How?"

"You can be a witness."

"Witness? But I was nowhere near when the incident took place," I said, a little bemused.

"Sir, I'm asking you to be a witness in court. So what if you were not actually a witness when it happened?" he said, smiling.

It was as if he was mocking the law. Doing something wrong is one thing, but doing wrong and being amused by it, is totally ridiculous. Such people who smile away their wrong doings, or those who justify it, put me off totally. I felt like punching him.

"But isn't that wrong?" I asked, knowing that it was a silly question to ask him. Anyway, we were also trying to save Megha, though we knew that she was actually guilty, even if not intentionally.

He looked at Megha and shook his head.

"Well, I was not even in this city during that time. Will they not find out that I'm lying?" I asked.

"Sir, you leave that to me," he assured.

I was perplexed. Megha was looking at me. I thought about ways to prolong this further. I was trying to find loopholes in a lawyer's thinking.

"But the way you want it, anyone can be a witness. Why me?" I asked.

I felt that I had a good point, but he shot it down even before I had finished.

"Sir, you are famous now. You are known as a good person. Your company is known to be ethical in all its dealings. If you testify in court, it will hold great value."

I was stuck now; I had been pushed to a corner. There was Megha, looking at me with the hope that I would say "yes". And there was someone within me who was against me even considering such an option. It was a terrible situation to be in.

"Give me some time; I need to think about this."

He looked at Megha for a couple of seconds and looked back at me.

"Okay, let madam know when you are ready," he signed off and left.

Megha and I continued to sit there, with the few silent minutes that followed triggering off loud voices inside me – loud voices of confusion and perhaps even shock. Those loud voices were suddenly dimmed by Megha's voice.

"You don't have to do it if you don't feel like," she said.

"It's not like I don't want to help you, but can't we find some other way?"

"Even I'm not comfortable with you or anyone else being a false witness, but we really have exhausted all other options. We need to do this to be sure," she said, looking down with a sad face.

"Megha, don't be sad. Give me time to think. You do understand that this is such a difficult decision for me," I said, as I put my hand on hers.

She nodded. For a few moments my mind was transported to old days when our eyes met for extended periods of time, my hand on top of hers. I could sense that even she was filled with memories of those old days. Then suddenly, I pulled out my hand as I realized that she was no longer my girlfriend. I realized that time had moved on. But my life was probably still stuck there, somewhere in one of those moments, years ago.

"I went for a walk around the city yesterday. I enjoyed it," I said, trying to switch topics.

"That's nice; I will also take you around sometime. In fact, why don't we go tomorrow?" she asked.

My heart was beginning to get excited. "A date with my former love? A date with Megha!" I thought. I jumped at it.

"Yeah, sure. Let's do that tomorrow."

"What about your husband, where is he?" I queried further, anxious to make sure that she doesn't bring him along on our date.

"Oh, he's actually gone to Delhi for a few days. He didn't want to go because of all that's happening, but I persuaded him to go as there's nothing much he can do here. And there's still time for the next court hearing."

I was relieved. Later that night, after dinner, I sat down in the balcony of the hotel room. It was a cloudless night. Stars twinkled all around, as I gazed upwards.

My thoughts flew into the sky, into the vast expanses of the universe. I thought about the world that we lived in. I thought about the countless other worlds that may exist in the far reaching corners of the universe. I have always been amazed by the endless spaces in the sky. As a child, I had wanted to be an astronaut. I had dreamt of flying away into the sky – into the unknown. But perhaps, we can't fulfil every dream in life. And whenever I remember that childhood dream of mine, I stare at the stars and feel a sense of astonishment and joy.

As I looked up there, I transformed myself into the child I once was, long long ago. I saw the nearly full moon. I wondered what it would feel like to land there, in a surreal space.

Sometimes I wonder if those thoughts of mine – those thoughts of escaping into another world – were a product of the melancholy in my life, especially in the last few years. I wondered if they were because of being stuck in life. Perhaps they were due to being caught up in the past – in the unchangeable, irreversible past.

Chapter 41

The pleasant morning, with the friendly breeze, mild sunshine and all the warmth, seemed to me the beginning of something new, or perhaps the long awaited renewal of something old. Megha and I were seated outside a temple, after completing the usual rituals of folded hands and bowed down heads inside. I don't know why she wanted to go there with me, but I didn't mind it.

"What did you ask for?" she queried, as we stood up and were putting on our footwear.

"Nothing, I don't ask for anything these days."

"Why?"

"Because I don't get what I ask for."

"You will," she said.

That raised my expectations.

"Really?" I asked, looking at her intently.

Perhaps she understood what I meant and looked away. She didn't say anything, and that somewhat killed my hopes.

Ever since the day that she left me, my belief in God had dwindled. I had thought long and hard, I had often debated about it. But I hadn't found sufficient proof – if any – to believe in God as we define Him. Some people say that it's all about faith and belief, not proof. But perhaps faith and belief too need some oil to keep the lamp burning.

Or perhaps I wasn't capable of limitless faith. Even so, that day, I prayed. I prayed for her to find a way out of the situation she was in. I asked God to forgive her. I also asked for Megha to come back into my life. I begged to be reunited – forever – with my love.

"What was your prayer?" I asked.

"I prayed for your happiness."

I smiled. The graph of my journey with her had always resembled a kind of sinusoidal wave – up and down, up and down – except that it had more abrupt downfalls. In those five years away from her, I had thought that it would never shoot up. But the moment I saw her on the promised day, in my mind, the wave had turned positive again. And the pattern continued. I wondered what the final state of the graph would be. The wave had to end – either way – someday.

We went around the city to a few shopping centres and busy streets full of people. It was a Sunday.

"Don't you want to buy something?" she asked, as we were walking through another one of those busy streets full of shops.

I shook my head. I was never one to go shopping. Even when I did, I just picked up whatever I wanted very quickly.

"Okay. Lunch?" she asked.

"Yes."

"I'll take you to a nice Rajasthani restaurant."

Compared with the Megha of old, she looked a little down, expectedly. However much she tried to hide her fear, it was visible on her face.

We entered a cosy looking restaurant, which was slightly dark inside. There were small lamps that hung from the walls. The dim light and the exquisite art on display made the ambience excellent.

As we were in the middle of our lunch, I remembered that this was my first date with Megha since over five years. It reminded me of those memorable days when she was with me. Perhaps technically, this wasn't a date, at least for her. But I considered it to be one. I thought of asking her if she felt the same, but decided against it.

"Where are your parents now?"

"My dad passed away more than a year ago."

"Oh I'm sorry."

She looked at me for a while and then looked down at her plate.

"My mother doesn't talk to me now. She stays with her sister. All of them hate me for killing Shalini."

"Oh."

"I understand them. They have the right to feel that way."

Her eyes were ready to be flooded with tears. And they almost made my decision – those tears of hers. I had to help her. I couldn't imagine walking away with her in trouble. I wonder if anything in this world has greater power than tears in the eyes of the woman you love.

I didn't want to persist with the talk about her family and so didn't say anything for a while.

"How is the food?" she asked, after she had managed to hold those tears within her.

"It's really good. I like it."

"I knew you would," she said. During the course of many a lunch and dinner we had had together, she had come to understand my taste very well.

I kept looking at her on and off and she too was doing the same. We felt guilty to stare at each other, like we had done years ago, but we couldn't help the glances.

I wondered why she had come with me. Was she playing with me? Did her heart still beat for me or did she just need my help? I needed answers to those questions. I couldn't ask her directly right away, but I had to figure out a way to find out.

Outside, that old companion of ours had sprung to life again. It was the rain. The drizzle was on, as we came out of the restaurant. It rained on and off that day, much like the short bursts of romance in our lives. We decided to walk around for some more time.

"Did you think about it?" Megha asked, as we were going along.

"About what?"

"About being a witness."

"Oh yeah. If there is no other way, then I have to I guess."

"But do you want to?"

"That's a difficult question Megha, but I'll do it for you."

After a while she spoke again. "Do you still love me Raghav?"

I stopped walking. She stopped too. She didn't need to ask that question. I looked into her eyes and spoke.

"What do you think Megha? Do I love you? You leave me suddenly and come back after five years. You get married without telling me. You ask me for help to get out of trouble. You ask me to be a false witness to save you, despite knowing the kind of person that I am. And yet, I agree. You tell me Megha, do you think I still love you?" I gasped for breath.

I hadn't taken my eyes off her. She looked away.

"Thanks Raghav, I'm so unlucky to have lost you. I was a fool."

Finally, she had realized that.

"What's the point in regretting now, you should have thought about it before taking such a decision then."

"I did, I thought a lot. Maybe I could have acted differently; but then, life does tie our hands sometimes."

"Won't your husband be unhappy if he finds out that we are hanging around like this?" I asked.

She thought about it for a few seconds and just shrugged her shoulders. We were silent for a few minutes.

"If I become a witness, will it ensure your acquittal?"

"Yes, almost."

And we strolled on. That was an interesting date; it was a journey in itself. How many little journeys life is made up of, those little journeys of everyday life, those little journeys of mirth and trite, of love and parting.

Chapter 42

Back in my hotel room, I remembered that I had hardly thought about work for the last few days. I checked my inbox, and there were plenty of pending items. I didn't feel like doing anything, but my work couldn't stop. I managed to send a few replies.

I called Sachin to check if there was there something that needed my urgent attention.

"Hey, how are things there?" he asked.

"Things are okay."

"You met her again?"

I had told him everything.

"Yes."

"And...?"

"It's a little complicated, I'll tell you once I'm back."

"How long is it going to take?"

"Not sure, it may take a few days. Anything you need from me, anything urgent?" I asked.

"Well, let me see...," he paused. "Nothing that I need immediately, but I would like your inputs on one or two things."

"Yes, I scanned through some of your emails. I'll respond today."

"Don't worry too much, do it only if you have the time. I'll call you if there's anything that is critical."

"Thanks."

We talked for some more time before ending the call. Even though I had planned to work only for a few minutes, I ended up spending the whole night on it. I looked at one thing and it led to another, which led to something interesting, and it went on. I didn't realize how much time I had spent till I looked up at the clock.

It reminded me of the wonderful powers of concentration. Somehow I had managed to stop those thoughts related to Megha and channelize all my effort to what needed my attention at that time. Many a time we underestimate the value of unbending concentration, but it's such a vital ingredient of success.

But it also made me wonder if this is how life passes us by. Maybe this is how life drags you to where you end up. Something you read, someone you meet, an interesting chat, exciting possibilities or mere necessity, hasty decisions, a path you take that leads you down several others, and then one day you pause, only to become aware that your life has passed.

Megha called me the next morning. "My lawyer would like to meet you again today. Is that okay with you?"

I wasn't sure. "Why does he want to meet me when I haven't yet fully agreed to be a witness?" I thought. But I couldn't say no.

"Sure."

"What time?" she asked.

"Two?"

"Okay, I'll let him know."

"Aren't you coming along?"

"I'll come a little later," she said.

"Okay."

I had just finished lunch and was replying to a few emails, when I got a call from an unknown number.

"Hello."

"Hello sir, this is Shekhar, Megha's lawyer."

"Oh yes, tell me."

"I'm sitting in the lounge sir."

"Do you want to come up to my room? 804."

"Okay sir."

After five minutes or so, I heard a knock on the door.

"Come in."

"Thank you," he said, as he walked into my room.

"Please," I said, pointing towards the sofa, signalling to him to sit down.

I pulled a chair and sat down opposite him.

"Sir, I wanted to discuss another possibility with you."

"Tell me."

"It's good that you will be a witness for us, but it would be great if you can do something more."

"When did I tell him that I had agreed?" I thought. I let it be. "Of course, Megha must have told him," I told myself.

"What else do you want me to do?" I asked.

"Can you publish a story about this case on RS3?"

"What? Why?" My irritation was starting to turn to anger, but I had to hold myself.

"Sir, if you put up this story and state your account of it, it will certainly help our case. RS3 is known for genuine stories and for always siding with the truth. So this will make a really strong case. Once we create enough doubt, it is hard for the court to convict anyone."

I was startled. I was reluctant to even be personally involved in this, and now he was dragging RS3 into it as well.

"Well, I can't commit to that, I'll have to discuss with my colleagues."

"Sure sir, we do have time. The next hearing is still two weeks away. But please do think about it. This is a sure fire way to turn the case."

"Okay."

"I'll get in touch with you after a couple of days," he said, and left.

I felt a little anger towards Megha. "Why didn't she ask me directly? Why did she send only her lawyer?" I thought. I decided to confront her.

She came to my room later in the evening. She was looking very pensive. Her voice also sounded very low.

"What's the matter?" I asked, as she sat down.

"I'm just a little down."

"Why?"

"Well, my life's somewhat uncertain now, as you know. But even otherwise, this keeps happening to me. Some days I feel really sad. Some days I feel as if there's not much to live for," she said.

"We all feel like that at various times in our life, but there is always something to look forward to."

I had had the feeling that she wasn't too close to her husband. He was a good man and she respected him, but I doubted if she would ever love him. The words she spoke, and the way she behaved that day, more than cleared my doubts. I felt a sense of joy. My chances of winning her again had risen, perhaps considerably.

"I'm not sure what I want to do in life. Even if I get out of this, I'll still have a lot of confusion."

She was looking into my eyes, and I was wondering what to say. Somewhat uncomfortable with that moment, I stood up to fetch a glass of water for myself. She got up and walked outside to the balcony. I could see the shadows of the evening slowly engulfing the city, the bits and pieces of light that still remained somewhat representing the small fragments of hope that floated around in my life.

I took my place beside her, staring out into the city, maybe somewhere into the distant past and into the unknown future. She moved closer to me, her body almost touching mine. I don't know if she did it consciously, but it sent an uneasy shiver through my body, the ripples of that shiver meeting the undercurrents of my beating heart and invoking in me memories of that night of celebration of long ago when she had stood beside me holding my hand.

And I couldn't talk to her about my conversation with her lawyer. My anger had evaporated. I didn't quite know how to behave with Megha around. Yes, I still loved her. Yes, I wanted her back. But she belonged to someone else now. In those weird days, I sometimes felt that I should just leave. I wasn't enjoying the situation that I found myself in. But then, this was the only chance to win my love back. And so, I held on.

I accompanied her to the gate of the hotel and waited for her to find a taxi. I was about to walk into the hotel after she had left, when another taxi stopped just in front of me.

"Raghav," someone called out my name.

I looked at the face that was popping out of the window. It was Mr Ranjan. It had been more than two years since I had last met him. I walked up to him.

"Hello sir, how are you?"

"All right."

"We haven't met for a long time," I said.

"Yes. Why don't we have a chat? Do you want to get in?"

"Yeah."

"I tried to get in touch with you in the last two years, but couldn't reach you," I said, after I was seated next to him.

"Yeah, I've been travelling a lot. Anyway, you guys have been doing very well. I'm glad."

"Yes, we've been helped along by well-wishers like you."

"And, you've made a real impact, I must say, even beyond my expectations."

"Yes, we're in good shape."

"And, how's everything personally?"

"Normal," I said.

"You look at little bit lost, or maybe confused. Is everything all right?"

I was tempted to tell him my story. I was even tempted to ask him his opinion, knowing fully well, how adamant he was about never doing anything that's not morally right. But I held back.

"Yes sir, I'm fine."

We chatted for a few minutes, before I got out of the car.

"I'll visit you when I'm back in Bangalore," he said, as the taxi sped away.

Once again, I wondered what life was trying to tell me. Why did I meet him there, suddenly, after so long? Was I being asked to think again? Life never gets enough of the pleasure that it feels when it sees us confused. It forever endeavours to complicate an already complicated life.

Chapter 43

I stood in the balcony, sipping hot coffee. A hot drink is like heaven on a slightly cold night, much like the warmth that a friend or soul mate brings when life turns cold. I had been in Pune for a week now. As the hot sips of coffee burnt my tongue and made their way down my throat, I thought about how different my life could have been; how different it would have been, if not for that one cricket match.

At sometime or the other, life does bring us to the point where we have to make a difficult choice. And eventually, those choices determine the direction that we take and where we end up. The path that I was about to take now had the potential to be disastrous.

Though I had virtually decided to do anything to help Megha, the meeting with Mr Ranjan had made me think again. Everything I had done over the years, the reputation RS3 and I had built up was at stake, even if not publicly.

I took out my mobile phone from my pocket and looked at Megha's photo, which I had clicked a day earlier. I stared at it, almost bringing it to life in my mind. The familiar face that forever made me feel crazy, her piercing eyes and that infamous smile, all turned my thoughts back in her favour.

I had to do it for her. Or perhaps, I had to do it for myself. Whatever we do in life – even when it's for someone else – is ultimately for ourselves.

Some of us underestimate the effect of love on a person. Some of us who haven't experienced it, and some of us who don't have a heart that beats, cannot understand how people can be in love with one person forever. For such people cannot even fathom the unceasing elation that true love can bring, nor can they ever understand the depth of the agony that loss can inflict.

When you get a chance to redeem your happiness, when life gives you an opportunity to reverse your loss, you just forget everything else and take the only path that leads you there. It's very much like the reaction of a person who is in danger of losing his life. The only path he or she takes is the one that gives him a chance of survival.

And I made my final decision in that moment. I made the decision to go down the path that would rescue Megha from the pit, the path that ultimately, I hoped, would lead me to her.

I called Megha, as I was having breakfast next morning.

"Hi!"

"Hi."

She didn't say anything more, as if she was expecting to hear something.

"Megha, I've thought really hard about it, and I feel that I should do whatever I can to help you. Ask your lawyer to meet me; I have to know what exactly is needed from me."

"Thank you so much Raghav. We'll come and meet you right away," she said with a relieved voice.

They arrived an hour later. As we sat in the hotel room that day, her lawyer began to tell me what I was supposed to have witnessed on the day of the murder. He began to tell me how I should lie. Megha was recording the conversation for my reference.

"Sir, we have to play our cards very carefully. This is the plan. Please listen to the exact sequence of events," he started off.

"You will go back to Bangalore and publish a story on RS3. The story will go like this.

"You were in Pune about four months ago – January 18, to be precise – for a conference. You also attended a painting exhibition where you met Shalini, Megha's sister, who was one of the artists. You were impressed with her paintings and were keen to buy some of them. She invited you home so that you could see a few more of her paintings. You went to visit Shalini two days later.

"As you approached her house in a taxi, you saw Megha and Shalini standing near the gate. Before you could get out of the taxi and walk up to them, Megha left. She did not see you there. You could see that they were in a happy mood and that Shalini was smiling. You met Shalini, had a look at her paintings and decided to buy a couple of them. It was evening when you left. You called her two days later only for someone to tell you that she had died later that day, after you had left."

He gulped down a glass of water, before continuing.

"You felt sad and then forgot about what had happened. Then, more than four months later – that's today – when you were in Pune for another conference, you read about this case in a local newspaper.

"You read that Megha has been accused of killing Shalini, and both their photos are in the newspaper. You are surprised and shocked. You are not sure of the complete sequence of events that happened that day, but you are somehow sure that Megha couldn't have been the killer. You somehow trace us and let us know about it. After going back to Bangalore, you decide to make this into a story."

I just nodded all along, as Megha listened intently.

"I would then present this story that appears on RS3, in court. We will plan it in such a way that your story appears around a week before the hearing. It would be ideal to make it appear just before, but that could lead to some suspicion.

"This would be a big turn in the case. You have seen Megha leave when Shalini was still alive. According to the prosecution's story, Megha visited Shalini in the afternoon and left the city after that – which by the way is true – so she could not have gone to Shalini's place again.

"The only problem with this story is that Shalini's murder will be a mystery now."

"Won't they doubt that I may have killed her?" I interrupted him, fearing that the case could take a horrible turn.

"I was coming to that point. Though it may seem like you may be the only other person who could have killed Shalini, it will be impossible to prove. Even if the prosecution wants to go down that route, your fingerprints will not match any of those recorded on the scene. And, why would you come forward to testify in the case if you were the killer? Who will believe that?"

"Yeah, very valid point," I said.

He nodded, almost wanting to pat himself on his back for the legal expertise that he was displaying.

"I will request the court to allow you as a defence witness and the judge should not have a problem with that. You will come to court and repeat the same story. We will make everyone feel that you previously did not know about Megha being accused of murdering her sister, and that Megha and I were not aware of your visit to Shalini's house that day.

"There will be a few questions that will come up – as they always do when we make up a story – but that's what I'm there for; I will handle that."

I was speechless. What a fantastic story! I couldn't have imagined such a story. The sequence of those events could never really have occurred, simply because Shalini knew about Megha and me, and I would not have let Megha leave if I had seen her. But the world didn't know about it, and that's what mattered.

"What if someone revealed to the court that Megha, you and me met here in this hotel?" I asked, more than a bit worried that I may get caught lying in court."

"Sir, you would have already mentioned that you contacted us. Also, the possibility of the court believing you is very high. I will stress on the fact that you are known to be a man of values. I will bring to the court's notice previous instances when you (and RS3) refused to side with people who were in the wrong. And if this story appears on RS3, it will have a stunning effect."

He told me all the other nitty gritty details. It was important that both of us were in sync with respect to every minute detail: dates, names, places and so on. It was hard, considering that we were trying to create something that was not reality, but we tried our best.

"You do your part sir and leave the rest to me. There maybe things that I haven't told you about, but it's better to leave them that way."

I asked him a few questions and he had quick answers to each one of them. I was convinced that if someone found a loophole in his story, he would manage to nullify it.

"Okay, I will do what I can," I said.

"Thank you Raghav," Megha said.

I just nodded. She transferred the recorded clip to my mobile phone and deleted it from hers. I was supposed to delete it once I finished writing the story.

When you've lived by truth all your life, mouthing such a big lie is very hard. As I lay in bed that night, I was petrified. I imagined myself standing in the witness box in court and speaking all those words – words that didn't have an inch of truth in them. I feared that I would goof up.

They say that telling the truth is hard, but that's such a short-term assessment. We always think of short-term consequences, and long-term success escapes our head. They say that telling the truth is hard. I beg to disagree. Telling a lie is even harder.

Chapter 44

I flew back that night. It felt so good to be back in Bangalore. It felt so good to be in my office, in my cabin, after a few days in the wilderness.

"Dude, it feels like you've been away for so long!" Sachin said, as he walked into my cabin. Shantanu and Sandeep followed him.

"You told us that you were going to meet Megha and that she needed some help. What happened?" Shantanu queried.

"It's such a long story. Let's go out tonight; it's been some time since we had dinner together. I'll tell you everything."

I got down to work. I needed to catch up on so many things. I planned to take stock of everything that needed my attention, before starting off with the story. I sat there that whole afternoon trying to do as much as I could.

Later in the evening, inside my room at home, I played out the recorded clip from my mobile phone and began writing the story. My hands somewhat trembled as I typed out some of the most untrue lines that I had ever typed. Nevertheless, thinking about Megha, my hands moved enough to complete the task.

Visualizing a story is an important part of storytelling, but expressing it with the right words and in the right style is perhaps equally important, especially when it's complete fiction. But there was something that made that task of mine even more difficult; I didn't even feel the story. Even when a story is fictional, even when the characters are fictional, the feelings are always real. The story that I had to write had none of my feelings behind it.

But I thought about Megha and my feelings for her, and somehow managed to draw from those feelings to make the story sound real.

Since I didn't have any images or videos, I requested my creative team to create some media, paintings, illustrations, artificially made pictures and so on, around the story.

"So, tell us the story," Shantanu said, as we sat in a quiet poolside restaurant at The Waves, the newest five star hotel in the city.

I narrated it to them as if I had really witnessed everything. I could read their facial expressions of disbelief all along.

"I can't believe it." Shantanu was as surprised as I had been when I had first heard it from Megha.

"She didn't look like someone who could kill," Sachin said.

"Looks are deceptive," Shantanu said.

All of us looked at him, surprised at what he said.

"Sorry, I didn't actually mean that. It was just a general statement," he said.

"She didn't do it on purpose, it just happened. But even I was shocked when she told me about it."

"Why didn't you tell us earlier? You met her in Pune even before she came to meet you here?" Sachin asked.

"Yes, I had tried to talk to her, but she had only told me that she would meet me later as promised."

It was in line with the made-up story that I was to present in court. Maybe I had become really good at telling stories over the years. I silently smiled at myself. I didn't realize that all those stories I had told before were real stories.

As expected, they had plenty of questions. "Why did you not try to follow Megha?" "Why did you not ask Shalini about her?" "Did Shalini not know about Megha and you?" But the important thing was that none of them expressed any doubts about the case.

I answered all their questions and managed to convince them. I had to make them believe my story so that it could appear on RS3. Deep down inside me, I felt a great sorrow for lying to my dear friends. But the wave had completely taken hold of me. It was dragging me down the path that I would never have wanted to go on; but I did.

And somewhere along the line I began to feel that telling a lie was not so hard after all!

A couple of days later, at night, I sat with the completed story in front of my screen, waiting to click "publish". The somewhat calm city outside and the noisy voices within me were a strange combination. What happens when calm meets turbulence? How does it feel at that exact point where silence meets bedlam? Maybe I had experienced it. Perhaps all of us have, at some point in our lives.

My hand hesitated for a bit, but I closed my eyes and pushed the button. And I visualized the bytes of that story travelling from my computer to various servers, to other computers and to the people. RS3 had its first false story.

I made it the main story for the next day and it remained in a prominent position for a few days. Stories written by one of the founding members always got more eyeballs and responses. In fact, it went on to become one of the most talked about stories on RS3. And unsurprisingly, it made some news in the television and print media as well.

Sachin came to my cabin the next evening, just as I was about to leave.

"I want to talk to you about something," he said.

"Tell me."

"Let's go outside to the terrace."

We walked slowly up the stairs, to the terrace. The evening weather was perfect for a candid talk with a friend. It was another five minutes before Sachin began to speak.

"Something is bothering me."

"What's that? Tell me."

"I hope you don't feel bad."

"Sachin, you can talk to me about anything. You are my closest friend, and I'll never feel bad."

"In all the years that we've known each other, I've come to understand you very well."

He paused, and I looked at him.

"That story you told us, about Megha and her sister, and you being a witness..."

"What about it?" I asked.

"Are you sure about all that you told us?"

"Yes, why? I didn't understand that question."

"I mean, I have a feeling that there isn't complete truth in it."

"Huh?" I was surprised and a little worried.

"Raghav, as I said, I know you so well. I know you don't usually lie to us, especially to me. But I feel that you are hiding something," he said, with a saddened tone.

"Sachin..."

"I'm sorry if you have indeed told us everything, but it's also okay if you haven't. You can tell me now."

I didn't speak anything for a few seconds. He looked at me, silently asking me to say something. I knew that I could no longer hold back the truth.

"How do you know that I lied?"

"I could see it in the way you spoke. I could see it in your body language. I could sense it when you told us the story."

It's one thing to lie to a dear friend, but it's totally another thing to repeat the lie looking into his eyes after he has sensed what you've done.

I waited for a minute or so before speaking. "I accept that I didn't tell you the truth. I know that I should never have done that; I let you all down," I said, slowly, in a mellow voice, looking down.

"So what's the actual story?" he asked.

I had to tell him the truth. From the time I had told them that false story, I had felt really heavy inside. That evening, as I bared everything, I felt the heavy stuff flow out of my heart and leave me, as the lightness returned. I'm not sure if it's actually easier to lie or to tell the truth, but the truth makes you feel a hell of a lot better.

Sachin just turned and walked away, slamming the door of the terrace behind him. I hadn't expected him to react too kindly, yet that reaction of his was a little hard to digest, even though it was justified. Maybe I had taken his friendship for granted. We do that too often in life. We take the most beautiful relationships for granted.

I just waited there, somehow hoping that he would return. After what were forty long and heart burning minutes, the terrace door opened again. I knew it was him, but I didn't turn around, my eyes unable to look at him, my heart not knowing how to talk to his heart. He walked the short distance towards the edge of the terrace and stopped beside me. He spoke after a short silence. "I know that you didn't even expect this from yourself. Things happen, we do things which we know we ought not to have done. But that's okay, we all learn."

He wasn't looking at me; he was just staring out into the open. I knew that he hadn't yet fully accepted what I had done, but I also knew that there could never be too great a distance between the two of us.

That was such a relief to me, those words of his. We had had our share of arguments and disagreements, but we had never before faced a situation when one of us had done something that was completely out of line with our core values. I wouldn't even have been surprised if Sachin had continued to react with anger. But he didn't. He chose to pass it. He chose to understand that I was human after all. He chose to acknowledge that people do make mistakes and that it's okay to let go as long as they learn from them. I admired him for that. Every person we meet in life, however short or long the duration, has something to teach us. It's up to us to make sure that we absorb the lesson.

"I completely understand the situation you are in, and I am no one to judge what you have done or are about to do," he said.

I didn't say anything, but he could see that I was sorry; he could see it in my eyes. Despite that, I had to go ahead with the plan. I had travelled too far ahead on the path now to turn back.

Our hairs fluttered, almost synchronously, in the evening breeze that was beginning to turn cold. And somehow in that synced movement of our hairs, the gap that I had opened up between Sachin and myself – by keeping the truth from him – was closed. We were in sync once again, as best friends should always be.

Chapter 45

I flew back to Pune later that week to act out the most important part of the drama. But whether it was actually the most important part is debatable. The act is never the main part; it's the decision to act that clinches it. So perhaps the vital part was already over; I had already made my choice.

As I walked out of the airport, I was pleasantly surprised to see Megha there, with her smile. It was not yet touching those old levels of charm, but I felt that it was slowly getting there.

"How come you came?" I asked.

"Just like that. I wanted to be with you."

"That's nice!"

"I want to tell you something," she said, as were on our way to the city.

"Tell me," I said, looking at her.

"Not here, let's go somewhere."

"Where?"

"Anywhere, doesn't matter. I'll take you," she said.

She told the driver something in – what seemed like – Marathi.

"When is the hearing?"

"Two days to go."

"Are you nervous?"

"I was, but somehow, ever since you really agreed to help, I've not been feeling nervous at all," she said, as she looked at me with thankful eyes. "Hope you are not nervous."

"I am! But I'll manage."

"What do you want to tell me?" I asked, after a few moments of silence.

"I'll tell you, wait for some time."

She asked the driver to switch off the air conditioner and opened her window. Her hair fluttered against the wind, and I was reminded of those long drives of old. Those winds were perhaps the winds of change in my life, but whether they were going to usher in a bright and colourful tomorrow or show me another long tunnel of darkness, who was to tell. Whether they were going to set my life on fire or burn me down, who was to tell.

We sped along. It was an empty road, almost nothing on either side, except for vast expanses of land leading up to the mountains far away, and occasionally, small hills. Megha stopped the taxi near one of those very small hills.

"Let's walk up that hill," she said, pointing towards it.

We got down and made our way to the top. Though no one was around at the time, it seemed that people did walk up there, because there was a somewhat clear path, albeit a narrow and muddy one. Perhaps all the paths in life that lead to the top are rough. What's the fun in a smooth ride?

We sat down at the summit. It was silent, except for the sound of a passing vehicle every now and then.

"Raghav." Megha turned towards me and looked into my eyes. After a pause that almost seemed to have lasted a whole lifetime, she spoke those words again.

"I love you," she said.

"Huh?"

While I knew that she still liked me, I certainly wasn't expecting that. She continued to look at me.

"Even though I left you, even though I never kept my promises, here you are still willing to help me in tough times. You still love me so much. I couldn't help but fall in love with you again."

She rested her head on my shoulder, as I put my arms around her. The ever increasing speed of the wind threatened to blow us away, but we held on. I was super happy! In her jet black salwar and colourful dupatta, she looked like the Megha I had known years ago. It seemed to me that my life was finally getting back on track. Those five years away from her were melting away into an unknown place in my mind, to be only faint memories.

"You mean you didn't love me in all these years away from me?" I asked.

"I did. But maybe I had to fall in love again, because I wanted to fall deeper." She smiled.

"But Megha, what about your husband?" I asked, a little worried.

"I've thought about him. He's a nice person, and if I tell him everything, he'll understand. He knows that I don't love him."

"I've known what it is to lose a person I love. Won't it be hard on him? Is this even right?"

"Raghav, I really want to set things right. I want to undo the mistake that I did five years ago. And what's the point in holding him in this relationship, he won't be happy anyway," she said, justifying herself.

I didn't ask her anything more, lest she changed her mind. What a joy it is to win back your love! And I can assure you that it's even better than the first time that you found it. There's no doubt that happiness in life is much more satisfying if it was preceded by pain. There's no doubt that a low phase in a relationship makes the high phases even more delicious if and when they come, the height of the high phases being directly proportional to the length and depth of the low ones. There's no doubt that fulfilment is that much more fulfilling if it follows emptiness.

The skies were beginning to open up. The rain, the wind, the trees, the mountains, everything around looked beautiful. But love adds a sheen to everything that elevates beauty to another level. There's something about the wind and the rain that fall upon the cockles of a heart in love. There's something special about that moment that can almost make up for a lifetime of sorrow.

And we sat there, looking out into the distance, with the sparks that emanated from our hearts outshining the sparks of the evening light. That was the moment of our real reunion. Maybe there was a future for our love after all.

Chapter 46

I sat outside the court, in a taxi, as I waited for the hearing to begin. I didn't want the press to mob me with numerous, unanswerable questions. With nervousness taking over me and with nothing else to do to divert my thoughts, I began observing people around the court.

There were lawyers, police personnel, hand-chained convicts, friends and relatives with worried looks, people with faces that reflected the deep anxiety about their future, and I suspect, thoughts about their past.

I wondered how many of those people held an untold story inside them. I wondered how many of them had come there with a garb on, the garb that would never let their true selves come out; the garb that would sadly compromise the truth. Sadly, I was one of them, and I wondered if any of those people looked at me with the same eye.

And the external appearances people put on is not just restricted to the courts, it's the truth of life. People rarely show the deep thoughts and feelings that lie inside them to the outer world.

I'd been sitting there for nearly half an hour, when I saw Megha in the distance. She was accompanied by her lawyer and her husband. I lowered the dark-coloured window to see her more clearly. She spotted me and smiled as she drew nearer. Her lawyer had asked us not to meet in the court premises. They walked past me and sat down a little distance away. Megha was looking at me on and off, as the other two were discussing something.

We awaited our turn on stage. Waiting for something you desperately want is hard enough, but waiting for something that is totally uncomfortable must be the hardest thing on earth. The anxiety inside me almost killed me. I wondered if I could fast forward my life, past that day, or rewind to the past. I did it several times in my imagination. Time must indeed be an illusion.

I felt more and more tense, as my heart sensed that our turn was drawing near. It was understandable that I was on the edge. After all, it was the first time I was acting in such a play. Of course life itself is one long grand play, but that's another topic of lengthy discussion.

And the act was played out in court that day: the pre-conceived, carefully scripted act that made a mockery of truth and perhaps even justice. But justice is a strange word. I sometimes wonder where it is to be found. Is it to be found in nature? Is it to be found in society? Perhaps in heaven? Why do some of us seek it so desperately?

Some of those thoughts served to downplay the mistake that I made, and I chose to look ahead to my life with Megha. Her husband's appearance in court that day had made me somewhat uncomfortable. I was hoping that she had already talked to him about it. I knew that I was being impatient, but isn't five years of uncertain waiting enough patience?

There is sorrow in life. There is pain. But if there's one thing that gets us in the end, it's confusion: the ever changing direction of the wind that ruins our balance. Loss is one thing, falling down is one thing. But hanging in mid-air without being able to rise or fall is undeniably frustrating. Prolonged durations with constant signs of hope and without results bring unbearable suffocation. I desperately wanted to breathe easily again.

I had a great chance to win back my love. For me, there were enough signs that my life had turned for the good. But who was to tell that life wouldn't surprise or shock me with one more twist.

Chapter 47

That evening, Megha and I were seated in a small cafe, situated right opposite the hotel where I was staying. The gap between the lonely evenings I had experienced in her absence, and the ones we had experienced together, years ago, was slowly being bridged. It was almost as if the past was magically being brought back. And the vibrant and colourful streaks of love that had painted those days of long ago seemed to be reappearing.

"Thank you for everything Raghav. I'll always remember this."

I nodded. "I hope so," I thought silently.

We were fairly certain that we had won the case, but there was another battle to be won.

"Did you speak to your husband?" I was desperate to know.

"No, but I'll tell him soon. I want to wait for the verdict before I do anything else. It still weighs me down."

I looked at her. She was so adorable. In joy, in sadness, in anxiety, in tension, in relief and in every other emotion that she showed, she looked more and more alluring. She was irresistible in a way that resistance cannot fathom. I didn't want to lose her again.

"Can I ask you something Raghav?" she queried, after a long pause.

I wondered how she always asked me this before asking me the actual question. And, as it so often happens, I even came to love that habit of hers.

"Yeah..."

"How come you didn't find anyone else in five years?"

"Who said I didn't?"

"What? You did?" she asked, her face showing signs of tension.

"Yes, plenty of them."

"And?"

"And what?" I asked.

"Why did you come back to me then?"

"I came back?"

"Okay sorry, I came back," she said, now showing slight signs of being upset.

Her beauty always rose to another level when she got upset, and I didn't miss a chance to enjoy those kinds of moments.

It was true that I had met plenty of pretty girls. Many of them were good people too. But no one else had made me feel like Megha had done. No one else had made my heart sing like she had done. No one else had pulled the strings of my heart and torn them apart. No one else had made life seem so beautiful.

In those five years away from her, I had – in many moments of hopelessness – thought about moving on; I had had thoughts of finding someone else. I had even tried to, though somewhat unwillingly.

But true love happens just once. Some people have asked me if I wouldn't have loved someone else if I hadn't met Megha. That's a nothing question, for we are destined to meet the one we love. What I always wonder though, is why so many of us are not destined to stay with them. What I haven't been able to comprehend, is why life is so cruel as to bring us together, only to separate our paths in a way that they cannot cross ever again.

"What?" Megha asked, interrupting my train of thoughts.

"Huh?"

"You didn't answer my question."

"Which question?" I asked.

"You said you found other girls whom you liked."

"Yes."

"Did you fall in love with anyone else?" she asked.

"What do you think?"

"How am I supposed to know?"

"Megha." I held her hands. "Look at me," I said. Our eyes met. "Do you think I can possibly love anyone else? Can you look long and hard into these eyes of mine and tell me that you can find any other name in them, any other picture in them, other than yours?"

She smiled, with a tear to enhance it. And I felt that the whole world lay in that face of hers. What else is life, but smiles, tears and love?

I stood outside on the road as Megha sat inside a taxi and went away. I continued to look in that direction for a few minutes, longing for the moment when she would be back in my arms forever.

There was still a week to go for the verdict. I decided to stay on in Pune. I made a couple of trips to Mumbai for meetings and conferences. All along, my heart was filled with a tinge of worry. I had waited so long for Megha, and even though everything seemed clear now, every extra waiting moment was a burden.

Chapter 48

The verdict was as expected. Megha was acquitted. She called to give me the good news.

"Hi Raghav, I have great news. We won the case. The judge said that there was nothing conclusive to convict me."

"That's such a relief!"

"Yes! All thanks to you," she seemed excited after a long time.

"And, what next?" I asked.

"Give me a day to sort things out. I'm going to talk to Viren tomorrow."

"Okay, I'll be waiting," I said.

"Love you. Bye."

"Love you too."

Nothing was in my hands now. I had done all that I could do to help Megha. I had done all that I could, to make her feel for me again. I had done everything that I could have done, perhaps even more than I should have.

When we do something that's not right, we know all along – right from the first moment it is conceived – that this is not the path the best person in us wishes to take. But what we do not know and do not realize – till we have actually committed the act – is the enormity of the error. That day, after I had done my bit to save Megha, after all that dust in my head had settled, the clearer part of me began to show up.

Every good thing has the potential to be misused. There are people who find inappropriate uses for everything. RS3 had provided a platform to reach out to people, to society, in the hope that it would bring about a positive transformation. We had worked so hard to bring it to the level that it had reached, especially so because we had taken all the right paths.

And one fine day, a fool decided to abuse it. Ironically, that fool was me. As that thought sunk into me, I was greatly disappointed with myself. No one else – other than the people closest to me – may ever find out about it. The world may still continue to respect and admire me. External respect is good, but that day, I fell in my own estimation. Not just because I had misused RS3, but also because I had personally let down the part of me that had always stood up for the truth.

Whatever joys I had experienced in life, whatever pain I had experienced, I had always had a warm feeling inside me because I had led a good life. I had always felt good about myself. But that day, as those thoughts swelled up inside my heart, I didn't feel good; I felt a little cold. In the end, our incorrect choices always come back to haunt us.

But I somehow buried those thoughts – those burning feelings of disgust for myself – under the colours and dreams of love. I had to. There is only so much sorrow that a heart can take. In spite of the great success of RS3, there had been no dearth of sorrow in my life – there never is, in a heart ruined by broken love.

And I directed my thoughts towards Megha. I directed them towards the wonderful life that awaited me. That ideal and alluring tomorrow that I had always waited for, was just within reach. The bullet that had shot down my high flying dreams of the ideal life years ago, hadn't killed them. They had been lying beneath the surface, waiting for a spark to ignite them and open their wings again.

The return of Megha had brought the spark back. There was no doubt that losing Megha, five years ago, had driven me to work harder and had in its own way contributed to my success. But that kind of mental state could only have taken me so far. With Megha back into my life and my heart filled with love, happiness and more dreams, the potential to fly even higher and to reach another pinnacle was immense. And I recognized that, with amazing joy.

So I pushed aside those old sorrows and new disappointments and let myself feel the happiness that I was experiencing, the sort of happiness that had eluded me ever since that fateful day of parting.

Every moment of happiness, whether real or illusionary, has to be seized and experienced, and lived. For fate stamps down on our hands when we least expect it, and literally tears away every bit of joy from our lives. It crushes our hearts in a cruel, inhuman sort of way.

But there was something else that had bothered me in those five years, something that plagues a greater part of mankind at sometime or the other. It was loneliness. Yes, I had friends and family in whom I could confide. Yet somehow, I was alone.

And as I lay in bed that night, I hoped that it was the last night of that forlorn feeling inside me. I hoped that the next dawn would forever bury the ghosts of my loneliness.

Chapter 49

The first rays of the next morning brought with them a sense of expectation. It was perhaps akin to a person waiting to get his or her hands on the treasure after a long chase. Whether that final wait, replete with an endless sense of longing, is the best part – even better than the chase itself – is hard to tell.

I decided to visit a famous church on the outskirts of the city. Since Megha didn't respond to my calls, I sent her a message asking if we could meet near the church.

As I arrived there, the Saturday morning service was in progress. The church building was a marvellous structure. The tall, resplendent pillars that supported the whole fabric stood like proud soldiers somewhat at the edge of the hall. On each pillar were small panels that had verses from the Bible inscribed on them. The benches on either side of the aisle were well polished and clean. It was an old church, but very well kept.

I walked towards the centre and sat down on one of the benches, surrounded by people who were lost in the words of the prayer being said. I closed my eyes, and although I couldn't quite concentrate to comprehend what those words meant, they kept my mind calm.

It was followed by readings from the Bible and hymns and small speeches with messages. The service ended with a final prayer. Most people made their way out of the church, but a few of them continued to remain there, some with their eyes closed, some others silently reading the Bible.

I stayed inside for a few more minutes, absorbing the serenity of the place. By the time I decided to leave, I was alone; everyone else had left. What remained were small remnants of the gathering that had concluded. What remained was only a faint smell of prayers that had been said, of blessings that had been bestowed.

I strolled around the church premises for some time and came back to sit on the steps in front of the main entrance. The door was now closed and there was nobody in sight inside the pretty large compound space and beyond. I was about to call Megha, when I received a message from her. "I'll be there in an hour," it read.

It was a typically lazy afternoon, the sort of weekend afternoon on which you long to lie on your bed and dream, or go on a long, sleepy walk. But that afternoon, lazy as it was, was to contain the decisive moment of my life.

One moment, the few trees that were scattered around the church compound seemed perfectly still, as if they were part of a painting. But the wind picked up speed every now and then, as if to set that painting in motion. It reminded me of how our life stops once in a while, only to meet some destined force and regain momentum again.

But even in those moments of perfect stillness, the leaves moved – ever so slightly, almost unnoticeably – perhaps to indicate that a whiff of air – however small, however insignificant – is ever present. How and when that insignificant whiff turns into a flurry, one never can tell.

I looked around at the deserted place, as thoughts of loneliness came back to me. Sometimes I wondered why it followed me. Or did I follow it? But I cast away those thoughts from my mind and reminded myself that new beginnings were around the corner, beginnings that I hoped would have no endings.

Sitting there, in the premises of a sacred place that afternoon, thoughts of the devil and sins came to me. Had I done something gravely wrong? Had I, in the madness of love, lost my senses? Had I slid down the slope that I had never wanted to? Was I, even at that moment, sliding further?

There is no doubt that it wasn't ideal to have turned into a false witness just to help Megha. There is no doubt that I shouldn't have used RS3 to further an untruthful story. And I accepted those errors of mine.

But love, as I have stated several times before, does that to us. What is love, if it doesn't make you lose yourself? What is love, if it doesn't impel you to make a few mistakes? What is the love that doesn't cast a fence around you and your beloved? What is the love that doesn't blind you?

And there's only so much you can dwell over what you've done. There's only so much you can curse yourself, especially so when life has thrown a few hard bricks at you – bricks that you feel you didn't deserve.

Life is strange. Sometimes it gives us lessons that teach us to be moral and ethical in our dealings. It also gives those people who have gone off track, so to say, a chance to redeem themselves. But why does it put those of us who are on the right track into uneasy situations? Why does it tempt us to cross the line? Why does it unleash the force of love on us and pull us even beyond ourselves?

My heart was restless now. I wished for Megha to arrive soon. I didn't want my mind to be clouded by any more thoughts of the distant or recent past.

The wind was no longer up and down, it had gathered a constant speed. The clouds above looked full, and it was certain to rain that afternoon. Only, I hoped that it wouldn't wash out my life.

Just then, I saw Megha walk in through the gates. I stood up as she came towards me.

"What took you so long?" I said, as I hugged her.

"Sorry, I just got held up."

"I've been waiting for nearly two hours."

She didn't say anything. I was still holding her.

"How come you are here?" she asked.

"I've been here before. It's so peaceful. I was feeling a bit uneasy, so..."

"Uneasy? Why?"

"Don't know. Maybe because you always make me wait. I hope you don't make me wait anymore," I said, my eyes firmly on her.

She shook her head. "I won't."

She sat down on the steps. I kept looking at her for a few seconds, before taking my place next to her. Dressed in a dull white salwar, she didn't look bright, but she was as graceful and as appealing as ever. In the wind and in the impending rain, in her beauty, and in the unseen force that connected us, I saw our future together.

But somewhere, I was sad that it had to happen like this. Sad that the road to our love, our future, had to go through by-lanes and places that we wouldn't ever have wanted to visit. Sad, that even in the fusion of two souls, there had to be a broken heart. But then, nothing's perfect in life, and maybe that's part of the charm.

"I spent a lot of time with Viren yesterday," Megha said, after a slightly long silence.

I set my eyes back on her in anticipation. She was silent again.

"Did you tell him? I hope he didn't feel bad," I said, knowing that the sorrow of heartbreak is even beyond feelings.

"You know Raghav, he's been good to me. He's always been with me, despite my indifference towards him. I respect him for that."

"I know. From whatever little I've seen of him, I can sense that he is a good man."

She nodded. "And, there's no fault of his in all that has happened."

In a moment – as if in a moment of madness, although not without warning – it started to rain heavily. We went further up the steps, towards the doors of the church, where there was some overhead cover.

"How did he take it?" I asked, somehow certain that she had told him. The sound of heavy rain was now almost drowning our voices.

"Remember, I had said that I want to undo my mistake?" she asked, not answering my question.

"Yes, I remember." I was relieved that she had remembered.

"But Raghav, I've realized that two mistakes don't negate each other."

"Huh? What?" I asked, somewhat unnerved by that statement of hers.

I could see her searching for words.

"Megha, don't talk philosophy; this is not a mistake."

"You don't think it is?" she asked.

There she was, talking about the philosophy of mistakes, after all that I had done for her. "Where was all this philosophy then?" I thought silently.

But I didn't have an answer to her question. Or maybe I did and was afraid to admit the truth.

"Over the last couple of days, in fact the last few days, I tried to tell Viren. I gave him signals, I tried everything, but I couldn't quite do it."

"God! I have to wait longer?" I thought.

"And I realized that this isn't right. I can't leave him. I shouldn't leave him," she said.

My nervous system almost broke down. My heart stopped. I heard the sound of thunder storms in my ear. The bubble – that rarefied bubble that I had slowly started to live in once again – burst.

"What do you mean, Megha? After all this, you are..." I didn't find any words.

"I don't want to make this tougher for both of us. The longer we are here, the longer the pain. Sorry Raghav, I don't think we are meant to be together." She couldn't gather herself to say anything more.

Megha means cloud. And Megha, the cloud, had opened up and submerged my life.

She got up, went down the stairs and took a few steps forward, as I also stood up. She was now drenching in the heavy rain. I was about to go after her, when she stopped and turned. She ran towards me and hugged me, her rain soaked body melting into mine, turning that moment of romantic melancholy into something truly unforgettable.

"Thank you for everything, Raghav."

She broke free off my arms, turned, and ran away. Before I could realize it, she was near the gates. I sprinted after her, the water splashing all around me. But I couldn't stop her. When I reached the gates, I saw her getting into a taxi, and she was gone. The chase that had begun more than five long years ago, at the cricket stadium, had finally ended.

I was horrified. I was shaken, even in the stillness of that moment. I stood there in the deluge of unending rain. The drops all over my face and body hid the tears that – without my knowledge – poured out of my heart and soul and merged with the rain water. The colourful ink on those promising pages of love was wiped out from the book of my life, much like the waves that destroy castles built on sand.

And in that moment of complete ruin, even with my eyes almost blind with tears and rain, even with my heart almost dead with numbing pain, I could clearly see the ideals of my life crushed in more ways than one. It was as if those soft, dreamy, well-intentioned pieces had been torn apart by choice and destiny. RS3 – and I – would have to live with a certain black mark – however private, however small, however passable – and Megha and that incredible feeling of love was now out of reach.

I never saw her after that. Yet in my dreams and in my imagination, she will always be near me, perhaps within me. Even now, years later, I feel the thunder of that moment around me. I still feel that final embrace. I still hear the cries of my heart.

For a few days, maybe even for a few months after that, I hated her. I was filled with anger towards her. But I slowly realized that living with hatred in my heart wasn't going to serve any purpose. And sometimes when I think of it, I feel that she perhaps made the right decision. Maybe finally, she had done something right. But that doesn't take anything away from the astonishing fury of the storm that it brought. It doesn't take anything away from the stunning calm that has accompanied my loneliness ever since.

Those were rainy days. Some days, it rained love. Some other days, it rained tears. It rained when we met; it rained when we finally parted. It rained on our hearts and on our souls. It filled the cup of my life with incredible moments that I'll forever cherish.

Megha was the destination that I had longed for. I didn't get there. But the journey, with all its ups and downs, and waits, with all its rights and wrongs, with all the delight and bliss and misery, had been memorable.

And I believe that our love lives on. Somewhere in those drops of endless rain. Somewhere in those sweet-stained moments of togetherness and tumultuous moments of parting. Somewhere in the unseen air. Somewhere in the endless sky. Somewhere along the bridge that will forever connect our hearts.

Samarth Prakash works with the engineering team at Amazon.com. Apart from designing large scale software systems, his passion lies in writing, born out of the longing to narrate stories that touch the heart. His writing style ranges from ardently melodramatic and vividly romantic to quietly philosophical.

A small collection of his essays and poems can be found on his blog "Misty Reflections" at http://blog.samarthprakash.com. Rainy Days is his debut novel.

Between The Headlines

The Travails of a TV Reporter

Shweta Ganesh Kumar

Size 22cm Rs. 125 176p
I.S.B.N: 978-93-806194-3-9

'Reporting for N.EW.S India from Bangalore, This is Satyabhama Menon'.

Satyabhama Menon is N.E.W.S India's latest entrant on Karnataka's reporting battleground. She is chasing stories with a vengeance, all set to get into India's best reporters league.

But is telling a news story on TV as simple as it looks? And what about Ram Kedia, the senior news editor and Satya's arch nemesis? Will he let her work on the field in peace?

It's not just seeing herself on TV that's making Satya's heart skip a beat though. But caught up in the world of Devdasis and politics, maha-monsoons and grimy crime, will Satya get a chance to indulge in some romance?

For more on that, come join Satya on her journey as a TV reporter in 'Between The Headlines.'